Glen Chamberlain has won a Pushcart Prize, the first Gilcrease Prize for fiction, and the Rona Jaffe Award for both fiction and creative nonfiction. The Rona Jaffe Foundation named her "one of the six most promising women writers in the nation." She lives with her husband in Bozeman, Montana, where she teaches writing at Montana State University.

Conjugations
of the Verb *To Be*

Conjugations
of the Verb *To Be*

stories

Glen Chamberlain

DELPHINIUM BOOKS

HARRISON, NEW YORK • ENCINO, CALIFORNIA

Book design and title page photograph by Greg Mortimer

Library of Congress Cataloguing-in-Publication Data is available on request.

ISBN   978-1-883285-50-0

11 12 RRD 10 9 8 7 6 5 4 3 2 1

These stories appeared, in somewhat different form, in the following literary magazines: "Amongst The Fields" in *Northern Lights* (Winter 2000); "Horse Thieves" in *Big Sky Journal* (Spring 2007); "Late Evening, June 14" in *Montana Quarterly* (Summer 2008); "A Mother Writes a Letter to Her Son" in *Montana Quarterly* (Winter 2009); "Off The Road; or, The Perfect Curve Unfound" in *Northern Lights* (Winter 1999), in Pushcart Prize XXV (2000), in *Montana Quarterly* (Winter 2007) and in the anthology *Ring of Fire* (Winter 2000); "Stacking," part one, in *High Desert Journal* (Spring 2011); "The Tracks of Animals" in *Montana Quarterly* (Winter 2007); "Tracks" (first version) in *Gilcrease Journal* (Fall/Winter 2004); "The Tracks of Animals" in *Montana Quarterly* (Winter 2007); "Twin Bridges" in *Big Sky Journal* (Winter 2005). My thanks to the editors for their early support and the showcase they provide for new short fiction.

For my parents, Glen H. and Milton J. Chamberlain,

who gave me love and a love of stories

I ate the day
Deliberately, that its tang
Might quicken me all into verb, pure verb.

SEAMUS HEANEY, "OYSTERS"

Contents

Conjugations
of the Verb *To Be*

Amongst the Fields

Outside the locked room is the landscape of time . . .
—Ursula K. LeGuin, *The Dispossessed*

Infinity

MISS BRETHWAITE'S MÖBIUS STRIP LOOPS ABOVE ME. IT IS A long stretch of butcher paper, twisted once by my physics teacher and then connected at the ends. She hopes that we will be able to visualize infinity when we look at it.

I can't. This is because one side of the paper is waxed, the other not. I do not think infinity comes in shades of shiny and dull. Miss Brethwaite also joined the ends of the strip with big staples. I do not imagine infinity being held together by tin stitches. Nor would there be a world around it that pulses, as the long fluorescent lights in this classroom do. I know that stars pulse, and being partially made of stardust, I pulse, but I do not believe infinity would. Certainly such a thing is beyond that, beyond the stars and me.

Below the ceiling, the air made warm by the clanking hot-water heater swirls around the twisted paper, fluttering it. Hanging since Christmas, its sides have become as worn as the edges of the road my school bus travels every morning and afternoon. In the spring, when the fog thickens on the long curve that twists up and over Buckle Summit and the borrow ditches beckon just off the slippery tar, I think I am closer to infinity than Miss Brethwaite's Möbius strip will ever take me.

Perhaps my lack of understanding stems from my familiarity with butcher paper. At least once a year I twist and tape patches of it around the specific muscles of a dead animal. It happens in early summer when Daddy, with a bucket of grain, leads the steer, still pulsing in hide and hoof, out into the lower hay meadow. He puts the black pail down and walks away. The yearling, a little spooky, walks up to it and blows, and the grain flies out. He sniffs and snorts and soon commences to eat as Daddy walks farther and farther away. About the time the steer's done, Daddy has found a spot to sit. He rests his elbows on his knees, his rifle in his hands, and he wrinkles an eye into the crosshairs of his scope, shrinking distance. I stand far to the side of him, wondering if time shortens when space does, and when I see his trigger arm tense, I hold my breath.

The steer crumples at the same time there is a hollow pop. The Angus is no longer in a gentle summer day, enjoying a certain bucket of oats. Though he is lying amongst the green timothy and the wild iris of my little meadow, he has entered another field, as well. All that really remains of him here is tenderloin and T-bone and sirloin and roast.

I look away from the Möbius strip and down to my wrist, which calmly beats the rhythm of my life. I press my thumb to that pulse, wondering how long it will be till I abdicate to infinity, and I sigh, not because I'm contemplating my end, but because I am having trouble with this physics test.

Phillip Steen, the dentist's son, hears me and looks up from the white space he has filled with tight little figures. It is impressive, this precise order he makes out of nothing. He is in love with numbers and with me. He has asked me out too much. But there is something wrong with his eyeballs. All the time they jiggle and bounce like they're attached to miniature rubber bands springing from the inside of his skull. I have come to think they vibrate to his brainy calculation of the world and of me. When I talk to Phillip, I try not to look at his irises because they make my head and stomach ache. I smile quickly at him and glance back to my own page.

Miss Brethwaite has said that it helps to draw pictures, that they will clarify the formulae necessary to apprehend the world. The particular problem that has slowed me involves a boat and a current. Sensibly, I began my illustration with a canoe and a river. As I've studied the problem, shrubs have grown up along the banks, and then trees—whole climax forests of them—have sprouted, and there is long grass that curls like birthday-box ribbon into the water where cutthroat run upstream and cobblestones run together. At first empty, the boat now has two passengers—men—and one of them is paddling while the other sits and stares at the ripples I have placed. It is Henry David Thoreau taking his brother, John, on the Concord and Merrimack rivers for a week, just before John dies of lockjaw. I think Henry should slow the velocity of the boat by not paddling, or maybe he should even stroke against the current. In such ways he will stall the arrival at his brother's jumping-off place. I erase the paddle and redraw it. Now it is poised above the water, and Henry and John float—just float.

I draw a little bubble coming from John's mouth and in it write the only thought I know of Heraclitus: "You cannot step into the same river twice." Just so simply the currents carry time away, and we are left confused by the velocity of our lives.

I look at my watch. There are twenty minutes left. I shake my head, for I cannot work this problem. In fact, I cannot work any of them, and the failure of a test seems as inevitable as the victory of currents.

With my head bent, I look up from under my eyebrows and glance obliquely at Miss Brethwaite, who paces back and forth in front of the class. She has snow-white hair and the profile of George Washington. She could be the father of our country except for her bosom, which is huge, like infinity. It juts from her, and she rests her crossed arms on the solid shelf of it. Her fingers, which drape over the starched yards of white cotton blouse, tap impatiently against the side of each breast. I think that there is so much endless firmament to her that the drumming must be inconsequential. I imagine her bosom to be like the universe, impervious to Albert Einstein's little fingers tapping on its wavy glass window. What did he see when on his tiptoes he first peered into heaven's cabin?

Forever, I think. Her chest. He saw Miss Brethwaite's breasts. And then I wonder if, when Miss Brethwaite was young, any man lost himself amongst her unbuttoned blouse, her uncorseted flesh, her immeasurable world. And could she remain impervious? She is, after all, an old maid. I wonder because I am just a girl. We have very little in common, Miss Brethwaite and I, except a curiosity about infinity. And what is that? Surely something more than velocity but less than love.

The Present

MAMA WAKES ME UP as she does every morning. "How early it is of late!" she whispers over me, and then she tugs on my toe as she leaves the room.

Early and late. I wonder if that is what the present is, a combination of the past and future. Do we need early and do we need late to have now? And what is now?

I look at the photograph on my wall, taken of my grandmother when she was sixteen—my age. It is an early version of her, not a late one, and her hair, curling in long heavy ringlets around her head, looks like black iron pipe. Because her gaze is demurely directed to the side, I have placed the photo so that the young woman in it looks shyly down at me in bed. From early in her life she looks out to late in her life: she looks at me. And

I look back at her. I think where our gazes meet is now.

In the summer, I have tried to catch the horny toads that live in the high desert west of Buckle. I wiggle my fingers in front of their upside-down eyes, hypnotizing them. As they watch transfixed, my other hand comes round from the side to grab their tails. If I am fast enough and nab them, their tails break off, and I am left holding just a pinch. The present is like a horny toad, I think. You can't grab it directly because it's too fast, and if for an eyeblink you do, all you have is a tiny dried scale of something already lost under the sagebrush world. I know every morning when Mama grabs my toe, she is grabbing the present we are in. It is transitory, and there is not a way to talk of it as there is for early and late.

Miss Brethwaite has told us about the Doppler effect. This is the principle in physics that says a sound coming at you is louder than a sound going away from you. I know it is right at that moment when the sound is even with you that you are in the present. It is when you feel most alive.

I know this by walking in the fields where Daddy keeps his horses. Often they straggle over to me, one at a time, and then stroll along. But sometimes they don't see me right away, so busy are they with their grass and each other, chewing on one another's withers, grooming each other's rumps, insulting each other with the slap of a tail, stomping on one another's hooves. Those are the times I like best, those when they don't see me.

I hurry by, purposely not looking at them. After I am well past, I assume one of them happens to notice me. Quickly the information is conveyed to the others. The conveyance is silent; it is not a whinny or a nicker. I suspect it is the long particular stare of the one that alerts them all, and soon they stop their business. In a bunch, then, they come galloping.

I hear them, their sound coming toward me, the pound of earth both hollow and full, the ragged breath that comes with running and the liquid snorts that come with excitement. They are all I hear, but I keep looking ahead, to where I am going. I move toward a specific riffle in the creek. It is the future, and known by me. And I remember that before they started, the horses were in the shade of the blasted but green cottonwood. It is the past, and also known by me. The sound of the horses gets louder and louder, and then it is upon me, the present, and it is deafening and dappled in gray and black and sorrel and bay. Then the sound goes away, into the future where I am headed. I love my father's horses.

"Miss Brethwaite says I will pass physics," I announce as I come in to breakfast.

My sister, home for the weekend from college, snorts. "How?"

I stare at her as I sit down. If she were not my sister, I would like her. She is lively and good at everything. She majors in literature and mathematics, representing both my mother's and father's strengths. I think when she was conceived, my parents still lived in the city, and the kind of marriage they had made them balanced. They leaned into each other evenly, like the two sides of an isosceles triangle. When they conceived me, though, they had moved here, to Buckle, and it was Daddy's choice, and they supported each other unevenly, like a right triangle.

I think when they made me, Mama was mad at him, so I am short on one side—my father's. She left that analytical part out to spite him. My sister received an A from Miss Brethwaite. "Miss Brethwaite says my work has been so interesting that I will pass. That's how," I say.

This is a half-truth. What Miss Brethwaite said was, "You write excellent science fiction on every lab report and exam you submit. If I don't pass you, you will be here forever because you are a moon-eyed girl."

I know what moon-eyed things are. I know because we once had a moon-eyed dog. His name was Moon, and he was a lunatic. When Daddy would go riding, he would get his saddle out and then go get the horse. When he came back, Moon would run to the saddle to guard it. He would not let Daddy near his own saddle. He would not let Daddy near him. Daddy would have to rope the dog and tie him to the fence post. He would come in laughing and say, "I have had to lasso the moon again."

The dog was such a lunatic that he could not take the sun. In just three years, his pale moon eyes clouded over with crusty brown pigment, and he was blind. Daddy put him down. He is buried up behind the house, where the deer run, because that is what Moon liked best to do—to chase them in some long, panting, unspoken now of a gully.

Daddy always buries our animals where they were happiest. Sometimes when I walk amongst the fields, I stumble on the indentations of lives lost under the sagebrush world.

The Past

"PHILLIP STEEN LIKES ME," I tell Mama. "Too much."

She and my sister and I sit around the old kitchen table, scarred by one of its previous users. Along with some old furniture, our house came with anecdotes, and we have cozied into them, both the furniture and the stories. The table, from the cookhouse, is signed by Lyle, who long before I was born blew his hands off with dynamite. He thought the fuse had extinguished, and he went to relight it. Afterward, he wore two silver hooks. Like some of us push our silverware around a table, he must have scratched away with whatever hand he wrote, and eventually *Lyle* appeared. His name floats on the table like a soul on a Ouija board. Most days I lightly place my hands on the name, wanting to ask the dead man questions, questions that have changed as I have. When I was little, I wondered if his wrists got colder in the wintertime, or how he held his horse's reins. But now I ask more adult questions like, "Did you ever dance again with a girl at the grange, and did she hold tightly to your hooks?" Or, "How did you button and unbutton your pants and your shirt? Was there a woman to do it, and if she did undress you, did you long to feel her flesh with your lost hands?"

As I trace his name with my finger, finishing it, preserving it with my own skin's oils, I look at the south-facing window, where another tale—one of someone my own age—is present. It is a long, drawn-out line slashed across the glass pane, wavy in its making and blued by its age. The sister of Lydia Pyeatt put it there. The story goes that a young man gave her an engagement ring with a diamond, but he was a cowhand, a poor boy, and she distrusted his ability to provide her with anything so pure. She took the ring and dragged its diamond down the window. That he truly loved her is proven in the etched glass in this house, day after day and decades after their deaths. Mama told me the story, as she used to visit Lydia in the nursing home. I would like to go see the old woman and hear about my house's past, but Mama says Lydia cannot tell me. "She has lost her mind," she explains. "Where do you think she placed it?" I once asked Mama, and she grinned at me. She thought I was teasing.

"How could anyone like you too much?" Mama glances at me as she slides a piece of lodgepole into the cookstove. "You are worthy of all the affection you receive." She does not use the stove so much for cooking as for the warmth it gives her. "You should be flattered that such a nice boy likes you." She quietly drops the iron latch on the firebox. "He's good to have in a crowd of kids. He's like the piece of green cottonwood you throw into the cookstove to calm the fire."

My sister and I look at each other and roll our eyes, in agreement for a change. Though we do not travel in the same universe now, neither of us is interested in boys who cool. We are after boys of willow or aspen—we are after boys of fast and fierce heat.

"Who do you like?" My sister has waited until Mama has left the kitchen.

I am not sure I trust her with the information. I hesitate. "Fergus Meagher."

"He is very hot," she says.

I am pleased by her response.

"Did you know he's named after a county?" My sister smirks

"He is not. He is named after Fergus, the fairy king in Yeats's poetry."

"I cannot believe you think that. His last name is Meagher, like the county."

"He cannot help his surname. He was born with it."

"But his first name is also a county. That could have been helped."

"That is coincidence."

"What is his big brother's name?"

"Which big brother?" I stall for time.

"The oldest."

"Lewis."

"And is that a county?"

"Yes."

"And his next big brother?"

"Carter."

"And . . . " She has the smile of victory on her face.

"A county."

"And the rest of the batch?" She makes them sound like cookies out of a cutter.

"Clark . . . Judith . . . Bonner . . . Dawson . . . Cassia. . . . " They are all in my state government book.

"Why do you think they have all those children? They must be either Catholic or Mormon." She is smug, for there are no Catholics in this valley. "I am sure that a Mormon couple named all their children after counties but for one. And they named him after an Irish Catholic fairy king."

"They could have." I say it without conviction. Instead of looking at her, I stare at *Lyle* on the table, quickly tracing his name, and then I look out the etched window at the falling snow.

Mama has come back into the kitchen. She is aware of the silence. "What are you girls not talking about?"

"Nothing," we both answer. My sister saunters out.

I watch Mama check the fire again, and I wonder if she married Daddy because he cooled her. I wonder because she is always feeding the stove. I do not think she married him for that; I certainly hope not. Though I would like to know her other than as my mother, she is no more approachable than Lydia, only she hasn't lost her mind. I think she has just lost her life a little, forgetting it in a city. Now, far away in Buckle, she cannot get it back. She should be more present, I think, present on a map—here, and on a clock—now. If she is not, how will she make stories to be left like old antiques, for someone else like me to someday polish?

At the beginning of the semester, Miss Brethwaite had Phillip roll a croquet ball one way while she tried to hit it with another, faster one. She kept missing, but finally she showed us Newton's first law—the law of inertia. When her faster ball hit the other, the one veered off and slowed down. This is because, Miss Brethwaite explained, the forces exerted by one particle on another result in the latter changing its motion, the magnitude of its speed, or both. Because of Daddy, it seems, Mama changed her motion and her speed. She was knocked off course to Buckle. I wonder if when she came to a rest and looked around, she was surprised at how lost she had become.

I would like to ask her. But I won't. "I am going for a walk," I say. "Do you want to come?"

She smiles at me and shakes her head. "It is too cold."

As the snow floats down in slow motion like the inside of a Christmas globe, I turn around in the air thickened by flakes to look at our log house. Against the gloomy day the rooms are lit, and outlined against the south-facing window, the one with the diamond line, stands Mama. Her arm is bent at the elbow, raised in a wave to me, and she is still, so still. Some of the room's brightness catches and gathers in the diamond scratch, and it runs a bright and sparkly diagonal across her shaded body, slashing it.

"Come with me, Mama, come with me." But I know she can't. She does not like the cold, and she is warm there, in the house Daddy has chosen. I am safe there, too, in the home she has made for me. But I know even as we love it in the same way, we use our love differently, and I will someday leave. Mama will not. Mama and the house will be my past. In a world made unfamiliar by its falling, I wonder at how we are separated—so transparent and pure—by a pane of glass and a line of diamond.

The Future

THE WHOLE FLOOR of Miss Brethwaite's classroom is a maze. Our homework assignment has been to bring a deck of cards. In class, our work has been to build twenty-six triangles in a line, the end of which connects with someone else's. When all the students' rows are completed, someone will be called on to touch one end of the maze, and then serially the whole will collapse. Miss Brethwaite says once we see the long, twisty, zig-zaggy line of cards fall in sequence, we will understand the particle-wave theory. This states that amongst any field, there can be a wave motion, and a wave is a propagation of disturbances, characterized by changes in the particles. The first disturbed particle creates the ripple.

Miss Brethwaite has threatened to fail anyone who accidentally starts the motion before its time. I look up at the Möbius strip, which has come undone and flutters, and I worry that the breeze in this tiny universe will dislodge one of the cards. When I look around the room, everyone is trying to be still, and everything is except for Phillip's jiggling eyeballs. I think Miss Brethwaite will pick him to start the motion, for he is her best student.

"Fergus Meagher," she intones. "Come here." As I watch him walk catlike toward the end of the card line, I am not very surprised. Of all of us, only Fergus could move gracefully enough to not destroy the experiment. In his pointy-toed and duct-taped cowboy boots with the undershot heels, he steps over the tediously built structure with ease. I watch the long denimed muscles of his legs, and I am glad that Daddy has told me it's all right to describe boys as beautiful, for Fergus is that. I am in love with him.

Apparently, Miss Brethwaite is, too, for it is an honor to be appointed the role of divine first mover. She is not impervious, then, to the tapping of human fingers on the universe, and I think how sad it is for her that she recognizes beauty she is too old to have. Her chance is past. Mine, however, is not. Mine is ahead. It is the future.

I glance at Phillip, who dizzily watches Fergus float above the city of cards. I wonder if he is jealous. Instead, he seems relieved that he has not been called to navigate this world, glad that he is the calculator, the accountant, rather than the god of this little universe. I could not ever marry Phillip, I know, because of his lack of imagination.

I hold my breath and look around the room. Everyone is doing the same, and all eyes, except Phillip's, are fixed on Fergus, watching him as he fluidly bends. Kneeling in front of the first card, his dark head is bowed, and I can see only the tips of his long lashes, but I know he gazes animatedly at the world of cards he will soon put in motion, for he is all willow and aspen. He is all hot and fierce heat.

He waits with his long, graceful finger extended. It is like the finger of God in the Sistine Chapel, just before he wakens Adam to the world, to Eve, to time, to the future. It is all potential. I can feel the anticipation like heat in my stomach.

Miss Brethwaite stands behind him, and it makes me wonder who made God. Could it have been someone like Miss Brethwaite, fulsome and white and separate, aware that beauty exists only if it is transitory and yet unwilling herself to be part of that transitoriness? She slowly bends over him, and the front of her white blouse, the part that shrouds her nipples, grazes the top of his head.

Miss Brethwaite says that this particle-wave phenomenon, also called destructive interference, operates in any physical system—gas, liquid, light. I am sure, then, that it operates in her. I am sure she feels his fine dark head graze those particular points of her breasts, which must be big as stars. He must be like a rock tossed into her waters, and the disturbance ripples through her being. "Now, Fergus. Now." She says it imperatively.

His finger flicks forward like a snake tongue, like an electric charge, and the world is put into continuous and consistent motion. I look ahead of the ripple, at the cards not yet touched, not yet affected or changed, cards angled into each other like the sides of isosceles triangles, like my parents once were.

In my geography book, there is an old photograph of a Japanese man holding on to a light post. His back is to the sea, and what he does not know is that right behind him is a wave, a tsunami, overwhelming and unstoppable. His future curls toward him, just an instant away. He will be like the cards that quickly go from perfection to right triangles to collapse.

I see the Old Maid cards I have brought, the cards for which I lost class points because there are not fifty-two of them. They are still intact. I look at Fergus's hands, which hang idly over his knees as he watches what he has done. I imagine his hands flicking toward my skin. I imagine the future.

Amongst the Fields

"ISN'T IT FUNNY how we deal with time so differently?" Mama says quietly. "People in the city want to buy it, and people in the country want to kill it." She bends down into the creek and scoops up another dead swallow. We are at The Narrows, a bottleneck of igneous rock that forms the entrance to our ranch. I am lifting swallows out of the creek, too, before the current carries them away. They are all dead.

Cal Rehnquist, a local cowhand for the Door ranch downcreek, has ridden through our property hunting cows. On the way out, he stopped to throw rocks at the swallows' nests. Mama and I, who were coming down from Silkey Bar after checking the irrigation pipes, saw what he was doing, and we ran at him, screaming like swallows ourselves. When he heard us, he mounted his horse and rode off.

When we got to The Narrows, the city of perfect geometric mud domes was a shambles, as if an atom bomb had exploded. Certainly Albert Einstein knew, I think, what practical applications his theories of physics would spawn. Look, after all, what a hand with a rock can do. Above us, the survivors dart willy-nilly like arrowheads without their shafts. Miss Brethwaite has spoken of the vectors of time, and these survivors seem like them. But they are uncontrollable, confused, and their noise is high-pitched and small in the vastness of this world.

When we have gathered all the swallows we can, Mama takes her shirt off and starts to bundle them. She has no brassiere on, and because I have never seen her naked in full and unadorned light before, her flesh looks fragile to me.

"You do the same," she tells me. Under my blouse, I am bare as well, so I hesitate. I am embarrassed, and ashamed that I am. Mama is busy with the little bodies, gathering them into her blouse, paying my nakedness no heed. I do as she does, laying my shirt on a rock and filling it with the tiny dead beings. "What are we going to do with them?" I am frightened that she is taking them home to bake in a pie, a swallow pie I could not ever swallow. I count the birds as I place them—two and twenty, three and twenty, four and twenty. How many does it take to make a sad, bad thing?

"We're taking them to the top of the rocks," she says. "They should be closer to the sky." We secure our bundles with a knot of the sleeves and quickly start the long crisscross walk up to the top of The Narrows.

Out of breath, Mama begins to lay each bird out, spreading its wings upon the pocked outcropping. They blend so well into the dark blue-black stone that they look as if they were in the sky when there was a big bang on the earth. Now they are a flock of fossils in flight.

When Mama is done, she stretches out on the rock amongst them, spreading her arms and closing her eyes. She is full bodied, I think, and beautiful, and I understand why Daddy loves her. Cautiously, I lie down next to my mother, far enough away that I can spread my arms out, too, but close enough that my fingertips touch hers.

When she feels my touch, she grabs my index finger and tugs it, like she does my toe in the morning. I feel her grasp relax and her muscles retract so that the skin of our fingers barely touches. "Miss Brethwaite says she is retiring after this year."

"Why?"

"She says that she has just learned of the law of singularity."

Mama's eyes are still closed to the sky. "What is that?"

"Miss Brethwaite says it is a situation predicted by Einstein's law of general relativity. There is an indication in his equations of an infinitely dense point with no dimensions and irresistible gravity. At that point of singularity, all laws break down. They all become fictitious."

"So?"

"Miss Brethwaite says if all laws are false, there is no point in teaching."

"I guess there is no point in living, either," Mama says.

I can see that she smiles, for the corner of her lips turns up. I do the same as she—turn my face to the sky, close my eyes, and grin. We should not be doing this, I think, lying so bare naked amongst the fields.

The Tracks of Animals

AT FIRST IT WAS LIGHT, THIS STARTLING AND DARTING OF wrens in the thicket of her chest, until Ada identified it for what it was. Worry. "Where's that Jack?" she asked aloud, letting the annoyance in her voice calm her, the question reminding her of how often she'd asked it. Jack did this too much, this "checking on things," this impatient walking about.

Tux, Ada's old border collie, cocked an ear and opened an eye toward her, thumped his tail twice, and settled back into his snooze. Smiling at him, Ada pushed another stick into the firebox, opened the flue to fan the flame, and then pressed her head against the window, scanning for Jack; she moved to the next window and did the same, and the next, and the next, until she had searched the four corners of her world. He came from none of them now, and the worry in her chest turned to something bigger, like a magpie lifting out of its messy nest, squawking. Fear. Jack should be back by now. And perhaps as easily as he walked into her life he would walk out of it.

She waited till the day was dimmed, and then she slipped her feet out of sheepskins and into snowpacs, slouched into her parka, and grabbed the flashlight. On the porch there was a shallow footprint, and a deeper one on the top step, another on the bottom, and then prints barely shadowed by the aura of window light. "Jack!" She zipped her coat up and turned on the flashlight. "Jack!" The light beam bobbled, illuminating and magnifying falling snowflakes in the dizzying darkness. With each bobble her fear grew. "This is ridiculous." She steadied the beam, casting it like a beacon into the vastness, a signal for him to come moor himself near her, at the table over a warm meal and then in their bed beside her warm body. But the sweep of her light did not find him cutting through the snow, pushing his way homeward. Ada turned to the door, opening it. "Tux."

The dog lifted his head to look at her and dropped it again.

"Tux, you come."

Her tone told him she was serious, so Tux groaned and shook off his stiffness. He walked under her arm as she pulled the door behind, hurrying him.

"Go find Jack."

Tux sniffed the cold air, hopped down the two steps, turned, and pissed on the porch post, watching Ada as he yellowed and steamed the snow.

"Come on." Ada riveted the light to the ground and

lengthened her stride to fit into Jack's prints. The static of night and snow enveloped her, each flake a point spinning into the tracks she was following. She stopped once to wait for Tux, who still stood at the cabin steps, watching her poke at the darkness with her little stick of light, and she thought of turning back and calling for help. But then she'd feel foolish when Jack turned up and everyone found out how needy she'd become. "You stay!" she ordered.

She hurried along, trying to outwalk the obliterating flakes, feeling breathless because she had never walked in his tracks before, and the strangeness of it let her see the world through his eyes: how small this place might feel to him after all he'd seen; what it would be like to hinge and unhinge long, thin legs and push through deepening snow on wobbly heron knees; how distant the earth felt under those turned-in-at-the-heel boots he wore; and she hoped her trespass into him would tell her where he'd gone. Somewhere between the house and the tar, though, she'd slowed and stopped, because his sign was snowed in. And she was snowed out, again just herself. "Jack!" she'd demanded, and then, "Jack?"

JACK DERITO WAS GONE. It was so simple that it defied her understanding.

Ada stood in the sun of a December morning. Its brightness belied the coldness around and within her. She'd been staring at the snow in this open stand of lodgepoles for more than an hour, long enough for her toes to ache with cold. She knew how white and clammy they would look against her hot pink nails, which just a month ago she had for the first time in her life painted. She told Jack their pinkness would forestall the encroaching monochrome of a Montana winter, even though that was a lie. She loved winter; it was Jack who grumbled against its length and paltriness of color. She had really painted them to be silly—something she had never been until Jack—and to please him because he loved her feet. More than any other part of her, he told her, he loved her feet. "Even the bunion?" she'd tentatively asked, for she did not like to draw attention to her flaws, but there was something compelling in Jack, compelling enough that she had done something even bigger than paint her toenails for the first time: she'd married him. "Even so," he'd answered. And he'd kissed her toes one at a time. Perhaps that was why he was gone. Perhaps a man needed to love more than a woman's feet to stay in a marriage.

Ada wiggled her deadening toes, thinking of how the lurid polish—now chipped—glowed like her life so recently had. She should go, she thought, go back to the cabin and run a hot tub and warm up and . . . and . . . live. But she could not take her eyes off of what was in the snow.

Coming out of the lodgepoles were small tracks—a vole, probably, whose rounded nose, propelled by its strong little hindquarters, had plowed the snow in front of it. Ada could follow the wake of its movement from shadow to diamond-studded light. She imagined the tiny engine driving forward in all this blank coldness, the heart firing so fast that it hummed, it purred, as with one little foot at a time it clawed itself right to its destiny, a destiny that was fulfilled right where Ada now stood. For at her feet, the lifeline stopped, just like that, and imprinted in the snow, lighter than air, was the swoop of feathers, the spread of wings and tail, the fossil of an owl.

"Why couldn't that have happened to you?" Ada asked out loud, and she was startled, not only by the noise of her voice, which for a month had been a mewling one of loss, but by her sentiment. She preferred Jack's death to her abandonment.

At first, she was sure that Jack had been swooped down upon, and for a month everyone else was, too. The search and rescue looked for Jack's tracks, they looked for the spent cartridges of a gun, they looked for strange license plates; and when that failed, they looked for the sign of an unhibernated and desperate grizzly, for the patient pugmarks of a mountain lion, for the wayward tread of an avalanche; finally, they just looked for some coincidence of fate. They found none. It defied understanding, this fact that Jack Derito was gone.

SHE HAD FIRST seen him in the mercantile store in Buckle. She'd gone in not because she needed anything but because she'd come to town to replace a muffler on the pickup and had to wait. While she ate a burger and had a malt at the Dew Drop Inn, many people she'd known her whole life came over to chat before they sat down with someone else. That she ate alone didn't make her feel sad—she had come to believe that with quiet one could hide from trouble, and the citizens of Buckle respected her belief—but it did make her feel separate.

When she finished her lunch that spring day, she walked down to the mercantile with the familiar awareness of her singularity, of her self-containment, of her skin. Out on the ranch, she felt no separation between herself and the world; she moved through it unmembraned, unaware of borders. Only in town did she feel the shape she had made of herself and, by consequence, her limitations. It was why she usually did not dally when she came in on errands.

But on this particular day, Art Samson at the garage told her the truck would not be ready till two, and it was only one.

When she walked into the store, Jack was standing near the cash register, squinting at slides he'd just paid for in the light from the big windows. It was his willed obliviousness, like that of an animal that knew it was being watched but chose to ignore it that made Ada want to study him. And so she stood on the far side of the greeting-card aisle, above the section marked FOR SOMEONE SPECIAL, and observed. She tried to be polite, just as she tried to be when she watched the wildlife on her ranch, occasionally glancing down, pretending that she was looking for a card. There were white tabs that denoted who someone special might be: FRIEND, said one; DATE, another; A WOMAN. A MAN. She picked a card out and opened it. "I need you," was all it said.

Holding the card, Ada discreetly watched the man as he looked at his slides. She imagined that he came from an ocean, for the one ear she could see was large with pearly folds spiraling inward like some kind of seashell. Ada had once been told that if you pressed your ear to a shell, you could hear the sea, and she had a desire to press her own ear to his, to listen to the tides of him. His cheek creased into a beard the color of Queenie, her sorrel mare, and she imagined how the whiskers curlicued back into his chin, his skin, his molecules, his atoms, his universe. The fingers that held the slides to the light were long and slender, and the nails were clean with little translucent moons rising at their bases. Ada had never seen such fingers on anyone, except an orangutan at the Hogle Zoo, in Salt Lake City, that year her parents took her out of state for her sixteenth birthday. When it had put its outspread hand to the glass, she had pressed hers against it and been embarrassed, for the ape's had been so much more beautiful. Despite that memory, Ada had a desire to walk up to this man, unfold his deft fingers, and, in the broad sunlight of the windows, stand palm to palm against him.

She looked down at the card. "I need you" was still all it said. There was a hollowness low down between her hips, which Ada recognized as desire. Up higher, though, there was a different feeling—an emptiness, but with a structure to it, like honeycomb, channeled and chambered. And sweet; she had never felt such sweetness. It was that sweet emptiness which made Ada understand that she had shifted from separateness to loneliness. It was what made her remember that loneliness was the same thing as love.

She stood there holding the card, watching it tremble with each rush of blood into her fingers, and considering what she might do. She put the card back, then looked up again at the stranger, who had put one slide down and was elegantly lifting another.

When her parents died in a car accident, Ada was just nineteen. What she had felt then was a knifing desolation. Sensing that such wounding could drive her from the one thing remaining of them—the land—she grimly set about befriending those she would need to keep it: the loan officers at the bank; the cattle buyers; the fence builders; the occasional hired men, never more than average but always young and unmarried and with bodies that could stanch (for a while, at least) the bleeding out of her emotions. At a young age, then, grief had given a task to Ada, which was to function from a solid mental ledge of practicality. This practicality, honed for a decade, proved useful now.

Again she reached down to A MAN, pulled out both card and envelope, and felt in her jacket for a pen. Under "I need you," she wrote her name and the directions to her place; her hand wavered as she wondered if she should include her phone number, as she had made it plain to everyone in Buckle that it was only for emergencies. But she was turning thirty and had never been in love; this was an emergency. "If you get lost, call," she printed above the number. After she paid for her card, "Excuse me," she said on her way out, reaching in front of the man to lay the sealed envelope on his box of slides.

Jack arrived that evening with a bottle of wine, and he was from the ocean. Or near it. He'd grown up in England.

"On the sea," Ada stated.

"Hardly," he laughed. He was from Warwick. "That's a good hundred kilometers from The Wash," he said, and Ada thrilled at the foreignness of him, that he thought in metrics and was so used to water that he referred to the sea as a laundry tub. "No, no," he corrected, explaining that The Wash was a bay opening to the North Sea. She brought out an old atlas that had belonged to her parents and opened it to England. "See Warwick?" He pointed to a dot in the middle of the country.

That evening, for the first time in Ada's life, a map came alive. The point that would have otherwise remained a meaningless speck took on color; it teemed with Jack, and his mother and father and two sisters who still lived within it; it filled with stories of his childhood; it spilled over into trips he'd taken to London, to the North Country, to The Wash, and even across the sea to Denmark. And once, he told her, he'd traveled to Penzance, the southwestern tip of the finger of England. He turned to the front of the book that showed the whole world. "Look," he explained, "look how this finger of land points to America," and he dragged his own lanky finger across the Atlantic, following the trajectory. "Landfall," he said, tapping Florida. "See how it's a finger, too? Do you know how in the Sistine Chapel God reaches his finger out to Adam's own sleeping hand, how he's about to charge him with life?"

Ada stared at the side of his face as he talked animatedly to the map in the book; she knew what a chapel was because right at the Buckle Summit was a little stone hut with a highway sign that told how it was a traveler's chapel where people could stop to pray; she knew what a cistern was, but she didn't know about sistines.

"That's how I felt standing at Penzance, imagining the coast of the United States, my homeland pointing me in the way I needed to go, charging me with life." He recounted how he decided then and there to cross over. He looked at her and smiled. "So I did a sea change, eh," and since Ada didn't know if he was making a statement or asking a question, she just nodded.

He asked where she'd traveled.

"Let's see," she said, taking the big book and turning to the index to find what page the Rocky Mountains were on. Her finger wandered until she found the place Buckle would be if it were only bigger. "I'm here." She tapped the page. "And once a month I go here." She slid her finger up and a little to the left, to Missoula. "To the Costco to get supplies. And then, when I was sixteen, I went here." Her sensible hand traced a path through river drainages and across a plain to Salt Lake City. "To the zoo."

She watched as his orangutan finger touched her own, which was still lit on Salt Lake, and she felt charged with life.

JACK DID NOT LEAVE that night. He had too much to tell her, and Ada had so much she must hear. Most nights of that kindled summer, after a day of making hay and before a night of making love, Ada would bring out the atlas and ask for stories. And Jack would

show her places he had been. Once, on a page showing England and France, he traced a tunnel—a chunnel, he called it—through which a train ran. She lay
naked next to him, trying to imagine such a horrible
thing. "You mean the ceiling of the tunnel is the bottom
of the ocean?" she'd asked. "Why doesn't it cave in?"

"Because the seabed's so deep between, eh. There's one
hundred fifty feet between the chunnel and the channel."

"Oh, my, I couldn't . . ." Ada so loved the light and
air—so loved her world of emptiness, which now, with
Jack, was a full emptiness—that the thought of the
damp, subterranean darkness covered over by deep,
dizzying water made her tremble. "For how far?"

"Right under this part." His finger ran from Dover
in England to Calais in France. When he looked up and
saw the look on her face, "What?" he asked.

"No. I just want to be here. With you." Her toes curled
on their own, one set of nails digging into the sheets, the
other into the top of his foot, and Ada was troubled, for
one foot cleaved to home, the other to Jack.

He studied her and then smiled. "I know." The map-
maker's pastel pages flew beneath his hands until he
came to Massachusetts, where he tapped almost before
he looked. "We'll go here. Boston." And he began to tell
her of the Mapparium, a globe of the world in a Christian
Science center. It was three stories tall, and she would
enter through the Pacific Ocean and leave through the
Indian without getting wet or seasick, and while she was
inside, she would stand on a glass bridge and look out
at all the continents made of stained glass and backlit by

thousands of tiny pinprick lights, like stars. "You'd be Archimedean!" he'd laughed in delight.

Ada understood him to say she would be a comedian, and though she wondered why her being there would be funny, he was so excited about the prospect that she didn't ask. For once he looked at her rather than at the map as he talked. "It would be a trial run before the real world, eh," he said.

That night, the Mapparium became for Ada the symbol of the world she wanted with Jack Derito, and it beckoned as bright and shiny as a great big Christmas ball. She imagined them, arm in arm, hayfoot strawfoot, leaving their prints on a world bigger than she had ever imagined.

And perhaps that was why Jack Derito was gone: Ada had gotten greedy.

IN JANUARY AND FEBRUARY, the snow fell daily. Ada would turn her face to the sky and feel the flakes melt on her eyelids and imagine how they floated all around her, millions of them, perfect and complete, and of how they piled one on top of another till they lost their shape, like bodies in a mass grave, and became just snow. She thought about how perfect and complete Jack Derito had been, and how perfect and complete he had made her feel for the short time they'd been together, and how their story had lost its shape, just like that, one dark November night. And though it was impossible after the three months he'd been gone, in the mornings and afternoons when she went out to feed the cows, she looked for some imperfect remnant of him in the snow.

One day, when she came back from her feeding and tracking, Earle DeCora was waiting, leaning against his sheriff's car.

"Earle," Ada said softly, her heart falling down.

Uncrossing his legs and straightening away from the car, removing his hat and slowly turning it by its brim, Earle nodded. "Ada." He smiled at her with embarrassment. "Could you tell me about Jack's run-ins with the immigration service?"

Ada shook her head. "Weren't any."

"They didn't want to deport him?"

"Well, they did because his tourist visa was up. But when we got married, they quit bothering him."

"When'd you and Jack get married, Ada?"

"August. It was six months ago on the tenth."

"And he left in November."

"No, Earle. Disappeared."

"Disappeared, then, in November. So you were married a little over three months when he came up missing."

Ada nodded. "But what's this have to do with anything?"

Earle put his hat back on, suddenly becoming official. "Ada, I was just talking to the immigration folks, and they were telling me that a person has to be married at least two years before they'll consider him an alien resident. Otherwise they view the marriage as a sham.

"Seems to me Jack might have thought two years was a long wait." He reached into his car and pulled out some papers. "Seems Jack had applied for an extension of his visa in June and didn't get it. Did you know that?"

Ada felt her skin move around the frozen ribs of her body like water, and she placed her cold hand on her chest to try to solidify it again. She spoke tentatively. "I guess I wouldn't be surprised. He liked America, wanted to see it all." She gestured to her land and lied. "Particularly right here. He said it charged him with life."

"But you didn't know?"

It was Ada's turn for embarrassment. She shook her head.

"Most of us would tell, Ada."

"That's because in Buckle, all of us already know everything about each other so we might as well tell. But Jack was . . ." She tried to think of a word to describe him. "Different." She listened to how unsteady her voice sounded. "We weren't just sitting still, you know. One of these years soon, after we sold the calves, we were going to Boston to see the Mapparium."

Earle's face disclosed nothing.

"It's a big globe, three stories of land and stars made out of glass and light that you walk into. To look out on all the world. It's what I wanted to see first and most of anything Jack told."

After Earle's visit, Ada quit looking for signs of Jack. Once a week she went to town; she'd do her chores and go to the library, something she had never done before, to learn of England and of the Mapparium and of Archimedes and of any other fact Jack had introduced her to, and then to find lives like hers in fiction. She was aware, as she made up her mind about what to take home, that her foot impatiently tapped. After the library, she went to eat at the Dew Drop Inn, where people, as they always had, came over and chatted and then sat down with someone else. Only now she didn't feel separate but alone. Terribly alone. And humiliated.

In March, the icicles hanging from the eaves began to melt, and she watched their tears drop onto the porch and evaporate. By April, the snow was receding from the cabin; she thought of the oceans and their ebb tides and of how they pulled back from the beaches—hissing, Jack had said—and she swore she heard hissing as the earth sucked in the thawing water. The ice on the tar went up in steam, and the snow in the borrow ditches, which with blowing snow and the detritus of the plows had grown taller than the highway, sank. All the way into town, a green ribbon of grass uncurled. And just beyond that, the spring uncovered the buried legs of roadkill. The stiff legs of deer and elk punched dainty hooves into the spangly air.

That was when a truck driver called in to say he'd seen a turned-in-at-the-heel boot on what looked like a human leg sticking out of the snow near Cottonwood Creek, a half mile from Ada's ranch. When he stopped, the ravens, a whole murder of them, flew off.

In the dead man's coat pocket was found the mail, more intact than he, from a November day—a statement for Ada Derito from the Minerals Bank; a bill from Mulkey Propane for 250 gallons delivered in October; a flyer for a pre-Christmas sale at the Buckle Mercantile; and a friendly reminder from the Buckle Carnegie Library that three books, all on the Baja peninsula, were overdue. That the man—Jack Derito—had been struck by a passing vehicle on a snowy night was assumed. Unclear was how it could have happened at the mailbox. Unknown was how quickly or slowly he died. Unimagined was what dragged him the half mile to Cottonwood.

When Earle told Ada that Jack Derito was found, he was shocked by her paltriness of feeling.

But paltriness is its own tapestry. Woven into it was Ada's realization that Jack had not stopped loving her; her understanding that she would once again have to save what was left—this time, though, it was she rather than land in need of saving; and her acceptance of the familiar comfort that turning away from wanting offered.

After Earle left, Ada sat in the grass, Tux leaning against her, his black-and-white fur warming in the spring sun. All around her, the world glowed, and it reminded her of the Mapparium. She thought of how Jack had told her she'd be Archimedean, which she now understood to mean that she would have been capable of moving amongst the relationships of the world. "Eureka!" Archimedes had shouted upon the apprehension of his sphere.

Ada remained still and silent, well aware of her place in the hopeful globe of green and blue.

Off the Road;
or,
The Perfect Curve Unfound

It was the geese that took me to that world without words. And that is how I came, for a summer, to be off the road.

It was May, and I was just leaving Three Forks, Montana, heading east on the interstate, wondering if it was those words the man had said that wrecked us. "I love you," he'd told me, and I sensed when he said that a devotion to language rather than to me, which meant an approaching breakup, a faithlessness. He was a writer, you see, and he spoke of how language should be like an engineer's curves—perfect tools by which to measure accurately. I liked his metaphor, and the fact that he ignored his goal of exactness when it came to loving me, that he used such a generic phrase to establish his affection, suggested that he was lying.

And so I left him, and I left Seattle, the world of our watery love, to return to another watery world—my home in Michigan. There I would live on a perfect curve of beach, placing my footprints in the sand next to no other footprints in the sand, a solitary figure needing nobody—no body.

In the late afternoon on the day I left for Michigan, I pulled into Three Forks to buy gas. When I paid, I picked up a pamphlet to read about the history of this confluence of rivers. It said that the Indians considered it one of the centers of the world, and as I drove off, I wondered if this was one of the centers, then where were the others? And how wise was it to have more than one middle to something? I knew enough about Einstein's theory of relativity to suppose it was possible, but, then, with his theory everything was possible. I also wondered if the Indians knew about the theory of relativity without ever having to talk about it, name it, get words into it, unlike my poet lover.

Given relativity, given springtime in the Rockies, and given that Three Forks is the place where the beating currents of three rivers come together to make the headwaters of the Missouri, I was willing to consider the proposition. And so I pulled off the road to a state park to see what it felt like to be in one of the centers of the world.

That's when the geese came. Out of the deteriorating sky, luminescent as candles in a vee, lit by the dying glow of day and the spark of inheritance that drove them north, they were flying homeward. I, too, was going home. But they were flying; I was fleeing. And they were going together, while I was alone. Once again alone, once again making the decision to leave before being left.

BECAUSE OF THEM, I didn't go back to that perfect curve of Michigan beach. I drove for an hour or more thinking about those birds, and then, past Livingston, with an easy turn of the wheel, I exited the interstate at a green sign that simply said CRAZY MOUNTAINS. With that turn, I forsook the one constant companion I'd always had— water—and headed north, north toward the mountains and the geese. I drove along a two-lane tar road for quite a while, crossed its centerline onto a dirt lane, and finally traveled onto two tracks. By then it was pitch-black, so I crawled into the back of my car to sleep that kind of darkness away.

In the morning, I awoke to snow. The world was as cold as my soul, I figured, and it made me feel good about where I'd gotten off, for I'd never spent time in a landscape that fit my personal geography; I'd always lived in lush, verdant places. Getting out of the car, I stretched while I looked around, and, seeing no one, squatted and watched my own warm waters, gathered during the night, dissolve the snowy crystals on the ground. And there in the dissolution, mixed amidst the pebbles between my shoes, were snails—lake or sea snails—empty and dry. I stood up and scuffed at the snow and dirt around me, where I discovered more and more of them, and then I went to look at a rock outcropping. Embedded in it were the same tiny shells, and imprinted in it were the fans of clams. I spun slowly around, looking at this white breast of a dim sea. It was a dead ocean, and it promised a silence I felt I wanted. Why, I didn't know, other than that it had something to do with love and its absence.

I got back in my car and drove on down the two tracks toward the emptiness, until I came to a faded two-story frame ranch house that sat beneath a cliff. When I knocked on the door, an old man answered. He was pulling a canister of oxygen and had a mask over his face. He didn't talk—he couldn't, because it would take too much of his air, I figured—so he just motioned me in with his long, skinny, blue index finger. Then he dragged his oxygen can like a golfer would his bag back to the La-Z-Boy in the corner; he sat down and watched me with eyes that, because of the mask, looked unnaturally big.

I watched back.

A long time passed before a woman came in. She was strong and handsome, a palomino-colored woman with big, strong, square teeth and a ponytail. Her name was Eleanor, Eleanor Tate, and she was the owner of this operation, she told me, and the man in the chair with the oxygen tank was Franklin, Franklin Coil, her father.

What did she mean by operation? I asked.

Horse breeding.

Did she need help, I asked, even though I didn't know anything about horses.

Yup, she said.

THAT SUMMER, I came to know horses—more particularly, Arabian horses. The distinguishing feature of this pedigree is not the spooned-out head: those are typical of the Egyptian—the third-world branch—of the family, which leaves the other side, the Anglos, looking normal rather than dinko-cephalic. Nor should Arabs be thought of as black, as kids' storytellers would have us believe. While many start out as jet as shoe polish, just as many within two years have turned a scuffed gray. No, the distinguishing features of full-blooded Arabian horses are their unpronounceable names (the whole stable sounded like a professional basketball team) and their short backs. Most horses have six lumbar vertebrae; Arabs have just five. That short-coupled back is what gives them their smooth gait.

The other owner of this operation was Bill. Bill Tate. I didn't know he existed until he opened the door one night—about a week after I'd arrived—and walked in, stomping the slush and mud off his shoes, for it had continued to snow. Bill was Eleanor's second husband, and over the course of the summer I pieced their story together. She was from New York State and had always loved horses. At some point early on, she had mixed up her passion for horses with her love of men and married one, a chemist who taught at the university in Bozeman. She said he cheated on her first, but I came to believe otherwise. Oh, she didn't have affairs; she just had a heart filled with thirty-five Arabs. I suspected that whenever her chemist tried to come close, he got trampled. Finally, he had enough and found a young coed with an empty heart.

After that, Eleanor took up with Bill, who had once been a dairy farmer in Maine, until his wife fell off a horse and died. Bereft, he sold the farm and came west in search of a new life. He found Eleanor, who really didn't want a lover but needed a hired man. If she married him, she calculated, he would work for free. He was a victim if ever there was one. That first night I met him I could tell, because his eyes were set far apart, almost on the outsides of his high cheekbones, like the eyes of deer and elk and antelope—the eyes of those destined to be prey. He was silent like prey animals, too, aware that if he made too much noise, Eleanor would find him and put him to some chore.

Of the three of them, I liked Franklin the best. Most often, he was in the La-Z-Boy, except when he dragged himself over to the moss rock fireplace, which Bill had built two years before; it was made from his very own harvest of rocks from one of his own fields, and as I came to know Bill, it became clear that this was one of his more successful attempts at agriculture. Once the rock hearth was in place, Franklin had taken it upon himself to keep the moss alive by watering it. He would stand there with his oxygen hissing and a little spray can in one upraised arm, pissing out at the moss that never grew. I greatly admired his desire to have a purpose.

I liked him for another reason, too. He liked my piano playing. The piano was in the basement room Eleanor let me use. It had gotten stuck down there when the house was built. Its first owners, who had come west right after World War I on the last and least homestead act, were so enthusiastic about free land that they decided to work from below the ground up, making the basement of a house to which they would add stories as they prospered. They put everything they owned, including the piano, in the hole in the ground and then built above it. When it came time to move their belongings up in the world, they discovered that they'd made the doors too skinny. And so the old piano sat forlornly below ground, ultimately as forgotten as the new dreams it once made melody for.

I liked to play it. I had never been very good, but I'd become used to my lack of talent and enjoyed picking at the keys. I don't think I ever enjoyed playing a piano more than that one in the Crazy Mountains, because it was so out of tune it made Mozart sound Oriental. In the concussion of East meeting West, I couldn't hear my mistakes, and it sounded so good. When I finished, I would come around the corner and up out of the tunnel of stairs, and at the top would be Franklin and his oxygen tank, hissing and listening. He reminded me of a fish out of water, standing on its tail, gills panting in and out, desperate for water, and there isn't any, and it is dying. Sometimes I thought a sweet clunk to Franklin's head with a stick would be good, except that he derived pleasure from moss rocks and Chinese music, and pleasure, I have come to know, in whatever paltry form, is what makes life valuable.

It was not long before my thoughts of mercy killing were ended. One June Sunday, a misty, moisty morning, I came back to the ranch from my day off. When I walked in the door and looked toward the La-Z-Boy to wave to Franklin (for I was becoming as mute as he), it was empty. Only the grease smudge where his head had rested and his air can with the mask hanging forlornly over its silver top valve verified that he had ever been there.

Bill was sitting in his chair reading one of his favorite Zane Grey books.

"Where's Franklin?" I asked, hanging up my dripping coat.

"Dead." He did not look up. He offered no explanation.

"That's it?" I asked. "Dead?"

"Yup."

"Where's Eleanor?"

He turned a page. "Ridin' Sad."

"Sad" was Sahid, Eleanor's honest-to-God black stallion, the one that didn't turn gray, twenty-two-years-old, her true love and her main livelihood. It was his color that brought mares from all over the country for a costly game of genetic roulette. If heritage spun out right, a new foal would be born black and stay black, and his name would be something like Sahid-al-Jasmine-al-Fed, and he would be worth $25,000 for his color alone. Eleanor hardly ever rode Sahid except in a couple of parades each year. She worried about him getting hurt. I had never seen her ride him, or seen her ride, so busy was she managing the herd. Curious, I put my coat back on and went out.

In the drizzle I walked around the house to the back, where the cliff was. It was a fault, really. The Crazies are full of them. A fault is a crack in the earth where two landforms are exposed when the world crashes against itself, crumpling, bending, pushing, and ultimately cracking. A cliff can be one of the results of this crazy self-destruction. The land leading up to this particular crack I was living under was shale, made of the old ocean bed, and the cliff was made of rich, soft, volcanic soil. It was up there, too, where Eleanor had her arena, the location selected because the ground was softer on the horses' feet. It didn't matter that it was windier and ripped the noses and ears off anyone riding her horses. The riders, after all, were just people.

At first I didn't see anything but an ink blot moving in the gray fog, kind of an animated Rorschach test. I moved closer and squatted along the fault line, watching Eleanor materialize straight-backed, riding that horse around in a prance, his front legs coming up in a high bend before snapping down elegantly. She rode by me, and I could see her back. In all that precision of movement there were big blotches of mud upon her coat from Sahid's hooves. The horse was now crossing the arena diagonally, his front outside leg stepping over his inside one while his strong hind end muscled him forward. He was beautiful. When he got to one corner, Eleanor rode him to the other corner and then crossed him back over the other direction, making a big X in the earth. After that, she posted a trot and made voltés, little circles, all around the perimeter, and then she disappeared out of the arena and into the fog. I could see the precise script of the horse's feet, a perfect geometric language signifying nothing. I had an inkling then of what it was like to live without words. I think I had come out to say I was sorry about Franklin. But Eleanor didn't need to hear that from me, any more than she needed words from Bill or from her first husband.

When I got back to the house, Bill asked, "Sad okay?"

"Yup," I said, and went to the basement to make imprecise noise on the piano.

The weather worsened that day, and by night there

was a terrible wind coming out of the east—a bad sign. When I got up the next morning, two inches of snow had blown in, turning the green world into a blank page.

Bill and I climbed into his old blue truck to go check his cattle—twenty-eight head of Hereford cows that were calving. Way out on a high meadow, we came upon a heifer that stood beside a still form in the slush. "Aw, Gaw," Bill whined, showing more emotion than he had for poor old Franklin, I thought. He jumped out of the cab, scooped the calf up, and put it on my lap, then punched out of the field as he headed for the house.

"El'nor, El'nor," he screamed, "it's a calf!" and Eleanor came running with towels as Bill carried the baby into the bathroom. He swaddled it, rubbing it dry, until the calf began to shiver. "There," he said. "It'll be awright. Leave it stay here an' warm up."

After breakfast, the calf still lay on the cracked linoleum, making no effort to move. As I cleaned my teeth, I was disconcerted by its big baby blue eyes, circled white with terror, staring at me. It breathed hard, and mucous sprayed out its nose; it was as if its whole body was filled with liquid that shouldn't be there, and little squeaks, like birds caught in a chimney, came from its lungs. That calf reminded me of Franklin, the way it looked and never spoke and the way it couldn't breathe. I looked away from it into the mirror, where I caught the reflection of Bill, who was filling a big dripper with whiskey. "Get down here and rub its legs," he told me as he knelt and squirted the amber liquid into the calf's mouth.

I clenched my jaw, and we worked silently together. As I sat there on a peeling bathroom floor massaging a cow while it drank Ten High whiskey from a crazy man and it snowed outside in June, I figured I had no idea what to say about my life. I was coming to understand the ease of silence.

After the whiskey, the calf's breathing bubbled more. "Don't wanna git the little feller drunk," Bill said. "Come on." He headed back to his chair and again picked up Zane Grey. I looked at Franklin's empty chair and the air tank and grabbed his squeeze bottle to water the fireplace. The world was quiet but for the sigh of mist and the hiss of wet wood burning. It seemed so foolish of me, so foolish of Franklin, to try to keep up with the drying elements of the fire, which had overcome any water in the logs and now crackled happily, the only happy noise in the house. The only happy noise. The only noise. The only. The . . . Words in my head were evaporating as quickly and easily as water when I heard a clickety-clack of hooves in the bathroom. Bill and I ran in, and the calf was still on its side, its legs galloping in a convulsion.

"It cain't breathe!" Bill shouted, and he loped out of the room, leaving me with the thrashing baby whose big wad of tongue, turning blue, was stuck to the floor. In a flash Bill was back, dragging Franklin's oxygen tank. He turned the lever, making the can hiss, and grabbed the mask, slipping it over the bovine muzzle.

The opaque plastic cup, which used to cover all of Franklin's face, just fit over the big pink nose of the calf. Its thin lower lip jutted from underneath, and the pastel ridge of its ungulate gums gave a faint promise of teeth, just like a human baby's. Pretty soon, the steady hiss had a regular rhythm, and the cow took its tongue back into its mouth. Bill removed the mask and gave it another shot of Ten High. "A coupla weeks of this, and the Nips'll want 'im," he said.

"What's that mean?"

"Kobe."

"What's that mean?"

"Beef."

"What's that mean?" I followed him out of the bathroom, but he didn't answer. I stood not knowing what to do. Through the living-room windows I could see that the sky was lifting, the sun filtering through the clouds, melting the slush, and the new grass outside was cartoon green. I felt an intimation of hope. But just then there came a long, plaintive cry from the bathroom, so I turned back to see what the calf was up to. Its skin lay caved in around its soft ribs, the oxygen all gone from it, air and life expelled.

We loaded the corpse into the back of the pickup and drove it down and away from the cliff, far out and onto the ancient seabed. There we lowered it down like sailors would a body into the green ocean of land for the scavengers to eat. On the way back through the shimmering grass, I thought about how that calf had died on bad whiskey and pure air. And that was all right. That was all I could think.

The rest of Bill's calf crop slipped with ease into summer, and then Eleanor's baby horses started coming, and the small ranch in the Crazy Mountains was like a miniature Genesis. It was all do and no talk for the most part, and it made me think of the Bible, how I never believed that in the beginning was the Word. I believed that in the beginning was the Deed, which wasn't invented; it was just done. The week the world started must have been a busy one, with light coming on and going off and water fountaining and land scaping and grass and herbs and trees and fruit popping and man and animals self-generating. There wasn't any time to sit down and put words to it all. In fact, it wasn't until years later, when Adam and Eve had to name the results of their deeds, and Abel and Cain theirs, and all those generations of begats theirs, that humans decided to write Genesis, and they lied, saying, "In the beginning was the Word." I felt myself becoming more and more like Eleanor and Bill, accepting that words were inaccurate and unnecessary. My longings for the poet lover became as dry and dead as the ocean that now grew fragile grass.

THE SUMMERTIME CAME and went, flashing a dusty green and humming a busy song as it passed. And when it was gone, the place was quiet. There were few chores for me to do, so I began to take walks, and I would look at the high autumn clouds like dapples in the sky, grass that cured and spiraled into thin air, aspen leaves that sparkled like meteors as they fell in the sun, and pine that wove itself into the shade of mountainsides. The world that early fall was like a giant lens, smoke-hazed from range fires and casting a filtered but intense light on everything. I waited and waited silently, for what I didn't know—the horizon to the north to burst into flame, maybe, and the firefighters to scurry on it like the freezing flies were doing on the spotted and indifferent rumps of Eleanor's mares.

The first cold snap came then, and the quiet pools of the stream glassed over, entrapping a late hatch in the ice. The little black bugs looked like print emerging on its own out of the middle of some old parchment, indecipherable. I didn't care that I couldn't read it, though, for I had given up reading along with speech. Total silence came when the ravens left, their barks no longer rising on the thermal currents. I was passive with the weather and the landscape, just taking in the particulars of that Crazy world, beautiful and finely etched as foreign script.

Though they hadn't said anything, I sensed that Bill and Eleanor wanted me to leave. There was, after all, nothing for me to do anymore. But their silence continued, for I had come to let them treat me as they treated each other—not overtly unkind, but indifferent. Since they did not articulate their desire for me to leave, I did not need to articulate my reaction. What I would—wanted—to do remained unknown because it was unspoken.

Then one morning I woke with a start of fear. Maybe they would never ask me to go. Maybe I would stay on forever as the crazy hand who sprayed the moss rocks in the fireplace and played Chinese music in the dark. With a momentary energy fueled by panic, I came out of my dark basement dreams, out of the dark basement, up the stairs, out the door, and into the dark dawn. As the black ink slowly washed out of the sky, I skirted around the cliff behind the house and up to the arena where Eleanor had ridden Sad, then down again and into the seabed field. My breath was shaky because I'd been running and I was helter-skelter scared, so scared all of a sudden, about becoming dumb. I felt unmoored, and I yawed around that land as the light changed from blue to yellow. There had been no blue to purple to red to orange to yellow, it seemed to me, and I sat down, winded, and wondered how the sky could go from one primary color to another. Given our invention of the color wheel, it seemed impossible. Then I remembered that I was living in a world that had not been overtaken by human invention. It just was. And that was what I thought I wanted.

I sat there frustrated and shivering, staring at the cured grass between my legs, and when I brought my head up, not twenty feet in front of me was a small blue rib bone. I stared at its blueness and its perfect curve, which made a parallel arc with the horizon. Crawling toward the rib, I saw the blue fly away, and the bone turned white. It's a vision, I thought, but it wasn't. It was butterflies, tiny blue butterflies, and at least five hundred flitter-fluttered off the rib into the yellow air. I knelt on the ground like a dog staring at a bone, and then I saw the other ones scattered about. These belonged to the calf, the one that drank whiskey and used up the last of Franklin's air. I looked around for my bearing, to make sure it was the right spot. Right spot, hell; it was one of the centers of the universe, a hole in that September morning air where different spaces and times came together and for a crack were measurable with a curve of bone and landscape.

I remembered that once, before I'd given up on love and words, I'd read the Romantics. I learned from them that you can't have continuous epiphany, a kind of spiritual orgasm. If you try, your life becomes mechanical, a kind of platonic sex manual where you put inappropriate tabs in improper slots. Samuel Coleridge tried to stay in an epiphanous state: it was an illusory place he called Xanadu, and he thought he could remain within its clear borders if he smoked opium. It didn't work, and he went crazy. Or crazier.

Maybe that was what happened to Eleanor and Bill. Maybe that Crazy Mountain ranch had been a place where they thought they could just experience things, like Eleanor's horses did, without talking, without trying to figure out, for instance, what the word love meant, or how to use it in the dialects of body and soul. Since they couldn't speak it, maybe they couldn't feel it—or anything else, and so they went crazy. Or crazier.

On that autumn morning, I knew I was crazy for having sought a place where words didn't exist. But I decided I didn't want to be crazier, so I went to the house and packed, and then I told them I would be leaving and tried to explain why. My voice was hoarse from lack of use, and my sentences were faltering. They didn't say anything. My words or Eleanor or Bill.

I haven't been much off the road since. In fact, I live in Bozeman, where I teach language arts at the university. The world here is not as pretty as that one in the Crazies. Nor is it so immediate, and at five o'clock on a weekday, its borders are fogged with sulfur dioxide, carbon monoxide, and ethylene—substances more dangerous than color wheels and language. I try to tell the man I love and the children we have borne about that pure and silent summer long ago, but the words fail me.

Stacking

1949

In the beginning was the world.

THEY WERE IN THE REALM OF GOLD, WHICH LAYERED THE world of green. It happened every evening at the same time, though if asked just when that was, they could not have said, other than a summertime when meadowlarks, after a day of yellow short-tailed business, sat on the posts of buck fences and quieted as the dusty sun leaned toward the purple sheeted bunk of the mountains. As the daybirds came silent, the boomerang wings of nighthawks began to whistle and drop toward the hay mounds, and the dogs, who had patiently waited in the shade of stacked grass through all the hot day of human labor, roused themselves and began to sniff and then dig round the loaves for the mice, which, disrupted from their nests and scooped up in the rakes and then lifted by the beaverslide far into the hot, curing green of timothy and alfalfa, scurried helter-skelter down the crisscrossed layers, into the digging claws and worn, waiting mouths of the dogs. Oh, it was a wonderfully hungry and full world.

The old John Deere tractor, which had pushed the windrows of grass onto the rack of the beaverslide, stood blessedly silent and greener than the summer land. And Dobber and Kate, the Belgians who all day had pulled the full slide up and then backed it down empty to the earth, again and again, waited dozing in their collars.

They waited for Holden Awn, still on top of the stack with pitchfork in hand, king of the mound whose grass he thatched and capped into a loaftop. Once shaped, it would bake in the relentless sun of August and then brown in the rains of September and the snows of November. And on some distant, dark, cold winter morning Holden could not now imagine, he and his father would break into this or some other loaf he'd shaped, and there would be bright green timothy heads and deep violet alfalfa blossoms, as summery as if the world was still all warmth and ease.

Though weary, Holden appreciated the cycle he had been born into. His arms were exhausted from pitching the hay and his legs were fatigued from stumbling through the grass that rained down from the slide; but now, working twenty-five feet in the early evening light, he loved the relinquishment and renewal inherent in his labor. Laying his last crosshatch, Holden stared with abstract admiration at the perfection of this small grassy world he had shaped, wondering if the mice the dogs devoured had felt pride in the grassy mounds they made. He sighed at the fullness of the moment and looked off to the north where the cottonwoods stood, their leaves purple and greasy in the dusk, their pale bark a glowing green. Just past them slipped the Buckle River, coppery in the fragmenting light.

The water made him think of the chaff, which wore him like an undergarment, and he felt encased and suffocating as he remembered Ingall, the hired man who in the fall would buy a new union suit, put it on, and not remove it until spring. Holden remembered how, on the first false days of warmth in April, the old hand would roll up the sleeves on his flannel shirt and then unbutton it and finally remove it; there the union suit was like a faded, stained, thinned layer of skin through which grew gray chest hair. And suddenly the boy's neck, his spine, his legs, his ankles, his arms itched with an intensity and desperation that only water could wash away.

As every evening during haying, he was to finish the stack and then lead Dobber and Kate across the field to home, but this restlessness in him, or at least on him, took precedence. Dropping to the seat of his pants, he slid down the mound. "I'll be right back," he told the horses, who stood with their heads drooped and eyes closed, each with a hind foot cocked so that the front of their hooves rested, for all their size, lightly in the beaten stubble surrounding the mound, and their shoes, exposed to the sunset, shone like overextended crescent moons. Each held a pose of patience and, it seemed to Holden, resignation. He shifted the collars on their necks, went to their faces, and with his thumbs wiped the crust of sweat and hay crumbs from their eyes, scratched quickly under their blond manes and turned toward the river. Tyke and Tuffy quit their mousing and followed.

Meanwhile, across the Buckle in her own family's fields was Emma Orchard, bent over a lark's nest— abandoned in a hurry by the looks of it, for there was a brown tail feather and a head's yellow down tangled in the twisted grass. She, too, had been haying all day, and now she was to be in the kitchen helping her mother get supper for everyone. Instead, here she dawdled, walking the meandering border of their land along the river, for she did not want to go in and do woman's work. As she walked, she imagined approaching the big old white farmhouse, which in the light would glow a soft pink, making it look more joyful than it ever was. Through the kitchen window, she would see that it was too bright and too hot with the electric light and the cookstove and the energy of her mother, which seemed unending even as it seemed exhausted. Yes, she would see her mother, whose hair had slipped out of its ponytail, moving back and forth, carrying a pot on one trip, potatoes on another, plates on the next, pausing to brush back the strands of her thick blond hair with a wrist, preparing so much food that the whole family would sink as much from weight as weariness into their beds; and in the morning, after an equally large breakfast, they would be so heavy that they could not fly away into the light blue summer sky.

And, she thought, that was all she wanted to do—fly away. But she did not know how or to where. She was unlike her twin brother, Emmet, who admired the perfection of woven nests rather than the ability of the nest-makers to flee. Emma did not understand his dedication to home, any home, their home. But then, she thought, the concept of place was so different for boys. She had listened at the dinner table, listened quietly as she sat across from Emmet while her father talked to him—only to him—about enlisting in the army, about enrolling in the state college, about seeing some of the world before he settled down to run the Orchard ranch, and Emmet stuttering and lying, "Yeah, maybe," or "That sounds good," when all he wanted to do was stay put. And when Emmet had pretended enough to appease him, their father would turn to her and say, "Only a year left till you're both done with high school," as if her brother's leaving while she stayed should make her happy. It wasn't that her father didn't love her; he just loved her so differently, and it was this difference that made her think that he could not love their mother in any romantic way, as a woman rather than as a hand and a cook.

She had said as much to Emmet that afternoon when they paused to watch their mother, who had worked alongside them all day, hurry off to start supper.

"Well, how do you think we got here then," Emmet had protested, "if he didn't love her?"

"Sex," she told him. "Just like the Herefords." And they had both grown silent thinking about their parents in any kind of copulation.

"You'd want to stay if you could run the ranch," Emmet had told her many times. "If you stay, I'll let you do it," he would offer hopefully, and, oh, how she loved her

twin then for his desire that they always be together and
for his belief that she rather than he would be the one to
go. "Besides," he'd always add, "you'd run it better than
me."

And she would, for Emmet didn't love ranching.
What he loved was this world that provided him with
bird eggs. For a decade he had collected them, climb-
ing high into cottonwoods and aspens and firs and up
cliffs, watching the zigzag flights of hummingbirds for
days and waiting patiently in meadows for larks to rise
so he could locate their nests. To their father's consternation, he would forget all his chores to find the dwellings
of robins, flickers, finches, sparrows, swallows, wrens,
chickadees and siskins and bluebirds and thrushes and
grosbeaks and hawks and herons and cranes and steal
an egg. "You're just like a magpie," Emma would tease
him. "Stealing eggs."

"But I never take more than one," he'd defend himself. And he didn't. Bringing it home carefully wrapped
in a neckerchief, he would forget more chores as he carefully pricked holes in each end to blow the small, bloody
contents out. In his room, on shelves he had built, his collection was displayed, each egg identified in Latin. For
the most part a sloppy student, he kept a journal that
precisely described the day he stole, where the nest was,
how it was constructed and of what, how many eggs it
contained, the sizes, the shades, and what the parents
did if they happened to come back while he was kid-
napping (he tried to make sure they were gone so they
wouldn't get upset). And if he could, he would always
bring Emma a feather from the nest. Though at first she

was not really interested, to please her brother she had made a scrapbook of them, identifying them, but only in American. Now, ten years later, it was one of her prized possessions. "Flight feathers. Bring me flight feathers," she would tell him whenever she placed one on a page, "and eventually I'll glue them into wings and fly away. Like Icarus."

"He melted his wings and crashed," Emmet would tell her worriedly.

"I won't," she would comfort him, feeling the older sister, which she was—by almost seven minutes.

Emma had just plucked the tail feather from the woven nest when she heard the barking of dogs coming from the river. She walked to the edge of the field, which abruptly dropped off.

Below her, on the far side of the water, were the Awns' dogs, Tyke and Tuffy. They had been swimming, and their shepherd coats now clung to them, making them look like little stick animals chasing each other in the shallow water, bubbles of spray floating behind them. Knowing they would not on their own give themselves over to such play, Emma looked for one of the Awn kids. It was Holden, and he sat on a purple trunk of driftwood, unlacing his shoes. He was going to go swimming, then.

Because he was undressing, Emma turned to walk away. Suddenly, though, she stopped in the stubble, realizing she wanted to watch and coming up with reasons why. Most obvious was the fact that she had never seen a naked boy, except Emmet when he was little. And then, of all the Awn kids, it was Holden who did the most with her brother. While he didn't seem as smart as Emmet or she, he was curious, and because of it, Holden had helped Emmet through the years collect his eggs. In addition, unlike Emmet, Holden had grown quieter as his voice deepened, and that made him mysterious. Perhaps Emma would understand him better if she saw him naked. And finally, she was so close to her brother that she often thought she was him. They were fraternal in the making and in their makeup, and yet what was expected of them was so different because of their anatomies. Exactly what, she wondered, was it about a boy's body that allowed him so much more freedom of choice? And so Emma turned back, dropped onto her knees, and crawled into the tall native rye grass that edged the mown field.

Having gotten his shoes unlaced, Holden was impatiently yanking off his socks, and then, without even bothering to unbutton his shirt, he pulled that and his tee shirt over his head.

Emma smiled as he stood and looked around to be sure he was alone. When he was convinced that he was, he unbuckled and unzipped his pants and peeled them off one leg at a time. Then he stood still in his boxers, apparently undecided if he would take those off, too. While she waited for his decision, Emma examined his chest.

Unlike her brother's, which had started to grow hair, Holden's flesh seemed as smooth, as girlish, as hers. And his legs, which because of their whiteness had a bruised tone in the manifold evening light, seemed hairless as well. The angular smoothness of him and the mottled quality of his skin made her think of a picture she had seen in a book. It was a sculpture Michelangelo had done of David, and the chest, arms, and legs looked polished and hard and stony and cool as the marble they were. That statue was so manly, she remembered, that she had been shocked by how small his genitals seemed, rather like a small flower on a thick stalk pressed into a nest of leaves. From the study of her own body, she could look at the sculpture and replace the leaves with pubic hair, but she had not been able to imagine the male anatomy of a boy, other than something somewhere between bulls and pressed flowers. "Come on, Holden," she whispered.

As if her whisper floated down to him, he gave one last glance around and then stepped out of his boxers. Now, before her, on the slight form standing against the luminescent geometry of the cobbled bank, what she saw was what looked like the small naked neck of a chicken. She squinted and stared, and its artlessness flooded her with a hungry wisdom.

"Holden," Emma whispered, neither in admiration nor in shock but in recognition of his familiarity to her, which now had a new dimension. Bemused, she watched as he waded into the water, watched his white stomach suck into his ribs with the cold of it, watched his hands clench as his arms bent and tucked up like featherless wings, watched his mouth shape an o of surprise, watched him dive into the current, watched him surface and hoot, watched the dogs plunge after him, watched the three small heads bob down the middle of something much bigger and stronger than any of them were. A little downstream he got out on a sandbar and did an awkward jig, then bent down for rocks and sticks to throw for Tyke and Tuffy. In between his tosses, he rubbed himself with handfuls of sand so that he looked aboriginal—powdery and pink in the changing light.

Again he plunged into the water, this time stroking against the current, going nowhere, the dogs beside him paddling, too, all happy in their timelessness. As the three played, Emma backed from the tall grass and then walked toward the trail that would take her down to the river and to the shallow crossing.

When she came through the cottonwoods, Emma slowed, taking in the whole scene—the balded meadow, the mounded green loaves proving its fertility, the silent tractor, the patient horses, the August sky flaring in the evening breeze. Nothing different, nothing out of place, nothing more than the austere but colorful world they lived in, nothing that said that Holden was any different from what he had been this morning, nothing to make him think he was any different, nothing except Emma. Summertime, seamless and ceaseless, suddenly felt to her to be finite and only cyclically balanced. She could walk to him and tip the world they had always known into some kind of motion by telling him what she had done and seen, or she could tell him nothing, and summer time would perhaps continue. For Holden, at least. She was now, forever, changed. As she walked toward the boy who did not know he was a man, she was aware, for the first time, of a power she had. It was not made of love.

Holden had turned away from the sunset to untie Dobber and Kate when he saw Emma coming across the meadow, her pants wet to the knee. All around her, the air was dotted by hatches of bugs swirling in gray circles and spirals and hoppers making black arcs above the ground and butterflies flittering blue into the dusk, which had gathered and now spread from the cottonwoods behind her. He thought of their wings, all of their wings, of how they beat against the air, displacing it, moving it, so that he could not tell what was in motion—the air or the wings upon it. All he knew was he could hear it, and it was abuzz. As for the earth, it seemed afoot, but it was not. It was Emma. Emma was afoot. He felt his skin, cooled by the water, flush, and the hot against the cold made him shiver, and his trembling embarrassed him, and so he blushed and shivered again.

Just as the wings of a nighthawk boomed and a kill-deer cried out, she waved.

"I haven't seen Emmet," he told her as she walked up. During haying, at day's end, Emmet was always in fields looking for nests, forgetting to go home.

"I know. Dad made him go into town with him to pick up some blades for the rake. I heard Tyke and Tuffy barking, so I figured I'd cross over and say hey to who-ever was still here," she lied. "It's you."

"I was down at the river." He flushed again, bothered to think how close she must have been to hear the dogs bark, how she might have seen him playing. "Giving the dogs a break." They were all too old to play, and he wondered why both he and Emma encouraged Emmet to still do kid stuff like hunt for bird eggs, why they both protected him. That was their connection, Emma's and his—Emmet. He tried to think of a time when he and Emma had ever been alone. It was only when one or the other was looking for her twin. "How you been?"

"Okay. I'm supposed to be home helping Mama with

supper, but it's so pretty I wasn't ready to go in." She motioned to the top of the mound. "Wanna go up? Watch
the sun set?"

He didn't. His skin was cool again, unflushed and
free of chaff. But she did. Emma. She. Not just Emma.
She. It was as if this girl was suddenly two beings. There
was nothing to differentiate her from the person he had
grown up with, other than that she had asked him to
watch a sunset with her. Without Emmet. For a moment
he felt guilty, and then he felt himself split, leaving the
boy who did not want to climb the mound below, leaving
his friend Emmet behind. "I'll go first."

Once on top, he lay down, hanging over the edge of
the mound and holding onto the tined end of the pitchfork he'd left stuck in the thatch. After she climbed a
little way up the slippery stack, she grabbed the end of it
and like a slow monkey reached one hand over the other,
moving up the handle, as she punched her feet into the
soft hay to gain purchase. When she got close enough,
"Grab my hand," Holden said, and as she did, he let the
pitchfork drop to the earth below. "Wait," he grunted
as he swung into a sitting position and she dangled and
hooted against the side of the stack. "Okay," he said,
and he scooted along the hay, watching her head crown
above the mound, and then her smiling eyes and face,
and her chest, and her free hand clawing at his cross-
hatching, disrupting it, and a crawling leg and then all of
her was on top. Out of breath and laughing—at nothing
but the excitement she felt—Emma stood up and did a
dance, then sat down next to Holden, who with his legs
out and his arms behind him, watched the muting land-

scape. The red turned to purple and the purple sucked into the shadow of the mountains until all that was left was a dark and jagged line between earth and sky.

"Star bright, star light," Emma said, and Holden joined her as she looked above and behind him, "first star I see tonight, wish I may wish I mighthavethe wishIwishtonight," they finished in a rush and at the same time, then, "OnetwothreeyouowemeaCoke." After that they were silent as each realized the lines of childhood had been delivered differently—there was no competition for wishes or pop—only flirtation. The world evenly blued out as the first star was joined by others, and just like that there was a coolness in the air.

"You cold?" Emma had felt his arm, which touched hers, shiver, and she thought how much more solid he felt next to her than he'd looked in the water.

"You want me to warm you up?" Without even waiting for him to answer, she crawled behind him and wrapped her arms around, tucking her head into his neck.

If he had seen Emma at all through the years, Holden had seen her as tough—tougher than her brother—and her arms around him confirmed that, but how small they were, thin ropes draping a portion of his ribs and knotted at his belly button; and then her chest, against his back, gave heat, but so tentatively that he felt if he leaned back to try to gain more, he would break her. She was like one of their kitchen table chairs, so fragile and rickety that he was afraid to move. And so he didn't, and slowly, he felt two points of heat, but whether they came from his shoulder blades or her breasts, which he could now tell pressed against him, he was unsure. This awareness—

that Emma had breasts and that he was confused—made him even more still. And so they remained, like statues whose bits of exposed flesh turned marble in the failing day, neither able to think of a thing to say.

Finally, from him, "I have to . . ."

Touch. Kiss. Go. Both thought of how to end the sentence. And neither could.

And so the snake did. As the boy and girl sat waiting in the darkening world for the right word to direct their actions, it was skewering its way out of the newly stacked hay, out of the breathless mound of growing heat and sinking gravity it had gotten raked and dropped into. Holden felt it first, on his hand, and the touch wasn't frightening. It was just long and smooth and warmer than he felt, and he knew what it was without saying so. Because he did not, could not name it, he did not move, but he did look down. In this end of summertime, the black and brown crosshatches of its back were not visible. Bull snake, he thought. And then he heard the whir of it, all abuzz. But in his innocence, he could not believe it. "Rattler?"

"What?"

1973

In the beginning was the word.

THE MOTTLED PURPLE SKY in the west darkened and dropped and settled on a row of old cottonwoods beyond the markers. She stared, and soon the trees turned black and the sky blued as stars poked holes in it, letting the light that had been displaced by the dark leak through. It was twilight, and it was a mood she was becoming accustomed to.

She did not feel so hopelessly dark as the quiet house she must soon return to, nor did she feel as optimistic as the light that each summer evening became a star. And so, what she was left with was her own life, small and growing, sometimes blocked, sometimes reaching out. Sitting on a pink granite boulder, Emma Orchard picked up a pebble and tossed it into the empty and effusive evening, seeing if at this moment her life was like a stone, or a star. Of course it fell to earth, onto the grave she now visited quite often and whose marker she sat on.

Bending down, Emma looked between her legs where the words appeared upside down, the words that enforced this transitory state, that made her question even as they somehow promised an answer, that made her seem fully but not quite herself. As always, the geometric print looked out of place on the rounded rock, which in the light glowed the same tones as her own skin, with a firmness and a softness, making her name, which had first been someone else's, look more like a tattoo than a chisel. Emma remembered how once, when she and Tre were younger, she had made her little brother copy the lettering onto her stomach. Above her belly button, in black Magic Marker, he had put EMMA ORCHARD. Below her navel, 1932 to 1949, and then in little letters, as a joke, **let 'er r.i.p.** When they had gone home, they showed off their handiwork to their parents. "Come here," their father told them both, and when they approached, he smacked them across the sides of their faces and stormed from the room.

If they had angered their father, he angered her, for, over the objections of Emma's mother, he had given her the name of his dead twin sister. She could never bring herself to call the woman an aunt, as that suggested a relationship, and yet it had been unspoken in her family that there was one—she just didn't know what it was. She did know that because of her name, she was supposed to want to leave the ranch, and she was to get good grades to receive a scholarship so she could; she did know that she was more watched than Tre, who without effort did well in school and said he, unlike Emma, would happily wave goodbye to the Little Buckle Valley in the rearview mirror. Yes, the name definitely carried a burden, and because she was saddled with it, at seventeen Emma felt that the name was hers to do with as she pleased. To try to figure out what that pleasure would be, this last year she'd started coming to the cemetery regularly to try to squeeze an answer from a rock.

It was not that she and Tre—indeed, the whole community—were ignorant of the story of the first Emma Orchard. Indeed, it had become one of those tales with a lesson, told to the young when they were out bucking bales during haying season. "Remember Emma Orchard and Holden Awn?" it went. "Just like rattlers used to get lifted by the beaverslides, now they get baled. Don't grab a bale without first checking."

Because it had happened in her family, though, because she had watched the sadness wash across her father's face, sometimes blowing in quickly, sometimes moving quietly in, sometimes circling for days like a front of bad weather, Emma understood that before the story became a lesson, it was an event as unpredictable as the weather. And perhaps that was where all stories came from—not from mistakes but from startling, insensible outcomes. And having known the story intimately, Emma always found the moral drawn from her father's sister's death an inappropriate one. It seemed to her the lesson shouldn't be about snakes but about something else, for what happened was when a rattler startled the young couple on top of a haystack, that other Emma jumped up and slid off as quickly as she could, onto the tines of a pitchfork.

She did not die immediately. In fact, Emma wondered if the girl had any sense that in an eyeblink her future went to being measured in minutes, for just one tine had punctured her, and as the illogic of the world would have it, that puncture was on the inside of her thigh, gouging the femoral artery. Before the story lost its blood and became a cautionary one about snakes, this was the full body of it: Holden Awn, whom she was not allowed to talk to—the father or his son—had slid down next to this other Emma, who laughed and cried at the same time, saying she had hurt herself on something. In the dark, though, they could not tell how red the hurt was, which streamed onto the side of a big draft horse he lifted her onto. Under starshine, worried for her and embarrassed for himself, the young man must have hurried the horse across the river and through the field, talking more and more as she laughed and cried less and less, her sounds draining out of her at the same speed as her life. By the time he reached the Orchard house, her heart still beat, but her veins collapsed a little more with each pump.

Emma tried to imagine worn Holden Awn as a young man, straight of back and unlined, probably as handsome as his boy now was, lifting her from the horse. One day, she and Tre, away from their father, did the math on how much lighter the girl was after losing all her blood. According to Tre's science book, humans had about ten pints. From helping her mother with the canning, Emma knew that one pint equaled one pound, so when the boy got her home and lifted her from the horse, she was ten pounds lighter. Ten pounds lighter, but dead weight. How did she feel to him? Did he know how hopeless it was? And Emma imagined her grandmother, younger than her own mother was now, relieved that her wayward girl was home, then not relieved when through the kitchen window she saw the blood smeared down the side of the horse, then worried when the young man carried her in, then terrified, then old. Just like that a life—no, two lives, or maybe the lives of two whole families—became stone.

"And that's that," people said. But they didn't know. They didn't live in the house where the story had drained itself out. What they should be saying instead was, "And that led to her," she thought; that led to this new Emma Orchard, a girl never allowed to be late coming home, a girl not allowed to talk to a boy named Holden Awn—a boy often just a desk away in many of her classes, a boy she had watched grow through the years into someone her girlfriends got crushes on, a boy she would like to have a crush on, as much because she wasn't allowed to as because she thought he was nice.

Sighing, Emma climbed onto her bike, pedaling quickly for home so as not to be late, believing that only she had a life so entangled with another's.

The pickup hurtled down the washboard road, its bed and a trailer full of hay bales that his dad wanted stacked in the river field. Holden Awn didn't slow until ahead of him he saw a silhouette on a bicycle riding into a bright circle of light, both circle and cyclist magnified by the lens of dust that hung in the orange July air.

Holden knew he should slow, but he was hot and tired and itchy and angry at yet another chore his father had dreamed up to keep him out of trouble, to keep him from going to town to cruise and drink beer. And it was Emma Orchard, who, since he could remember, he had been taught to avoid. His family, one of the biggest landholders in the county, was lower than no one, yet around the Orchards, he and Lucy had been taught to walk like cats— softly, watchful without appearing so, and with a wide berth. And all that effort worked. She never looked at him.

"To hell with you," he whispered and punched the gas pedal, watching in the passenger-side mirror, beyond the trailer, as the spangling orange was made heavy with road dirt that fell down around the girl. "Dust to dust." And then in the same mirror he watched the trailer swing out and then in and then out again, and the bales flying everywhere. Without thinking, he braked, and the trailer swung wider, flinging even more hay, and those bales in the bed, stacked higher than the cab, came sliding down over the windshield, bumping from the hood onto the road, where he plowed into them, exploding them, before he could stop.

Unbelieving, Holden sat in the cab and stared in the rearview mirror to see how much of his load was left. That he could see over truck bed and over the trailer, into the dust storm he had created and which now was enveloping the pickup, told him that he'd lost most of it. "Shitshitshitshitshitshit," he chattered more than spoke. He was already tired from bucking the sixty-pound bales into the bed and onto the trailer, and now he was going to have to load them all again—well, minus the ones he'd blown up—before he'd have to stack them.

"You sound like my cat. She makes that hissing, clacking noise when she stalks birds."

She startled him. She was right at his window, looking in, looking at him, talking to him, straight to him, just to him, to him alone and only. He had heard her voice many times, knew it well because he never looked at her in a classroom. Like a blind person comes to depend on senses other than sight, he knew her by her sound, knew how when she was called on by a teacher, she breathed deeply before she began to talk, not in any kind of resignation but in a gathering of air and thought and self, unsure but willing to answer up to something. And her *s*'s—she lisped, and so he knew that her tongue was a vagrant one, defying her the articulation she worked so hard at, slipping out between her teeth, which tried to control it, a cage of ivory holding a half-wild thing. She spoke in pauses but never in fragments, and the phrases always ended in an updraft of voice, as if her ideas were light enough to float round the world and come down just where they had to. He heard all this as he sprawled at his desk, his long legs stretched out and crossed at the ankles, the toes of his cowboy boots pointing defiantly at the ceiling, his chin sunk on his chest; he knew all this as he feigned indifference. Holden could not speak.

"Are you all right?"

"Yeah." He opened the door and got out, needing the space the road and borrow ditch would provide him so that he could avert his eyes, as he had trained them to do. And when he had looked around for as long as he could, he walked over to the bale farthest away from her and kicked it. And then he picked it up and started carrying it to the truck. As he neared her, he saw her gather herself just as he imagined she did before speaking.

"Why don't we load the ones nearest the pickup first? Then the ones near the trailer. Then we can back up and get the rest. Not so far to carry them."

"You can't help me."

"Sure I can. I stack at home all the time." She lifted a bale, testing it. "A lot lighter than ours."

Holden wanted to say that he meant something else, that she couldn't help him because he was an Awn, Holden Awn, the son of the one who some said caused her aunt's death. Though the story went that it was a rattler's fault, there had been whisperings about what the two kids had been doing on top of the stack in the dark. Holden couldn't imagine his quiet father doing anything. With anybody. In fact, he imagined his father lugging bales of quiet with him everywhere, never able to put them down, never letting anyone close. Holden wondered how he had found the words to woo his mother. Or had she plowed right through his stack of bales, like the truck had just done? Perhaps when his father left after the accident, joining the army and then getting a GED and going on to a California school on the GI Bill, he unstacked himself. Though Holden didn't fully understand, he knew that his parents had a kind of love, his father's a silent sort and his mother's a vivacious one. Maybe when he left, he would become vivacious, like his father was allowed to be away from here, and his mother was by nature. Like he was supposed to be right now, in front of Emma Orchard. "I don't mean that. You look strong enough."

"I'm almost as tall as you." Stepping close to him, she put her hand on the top of her head and then stiffly moved it toward his forehead. She could see her fingers trembling, feel her heart beating like hummingbird wings, small and ferocious. He held his breath as her hand touched just above the bridge of his nose, and as he felt her fingers on his eyebrow, his eye twitched.

It was not that boy or girl was innocent. Both had necked in the backseats of cars and in the cabs of pickups, each with town kids because it seemed less incestuous. Since they'd gone to the one-room Buckle School up through eighth grade, the thought of lying in a car with anyone who had attended class with them would be almost like Emma lying with her brother or Holden with his sister; there was a familiarity close to being family-like. And so, their freshman year, rife with hormones, the Buckle kids scattered, studying their new, more sophisticated town classmates, eager to embrace not only their ways but them. As Emma's hand barely touched Holden's forehead, though, they felt like the first couple of the world, as both, for all their lives, had been denied the countenance of the other. They were familiar with each other because their lands bordered one another, they were entangled in each other's stories for two generations, yet neither had ever gazed for so long or so close on the other. And so, in the tentative touch of palm to forehead, something bred of familiarity and foreignness was felt by both.

Holden pulled his head away and Emma her hand. "You are tall," he said. "I'm six-one." He moved to a bale, clasping it to his belly to hide his groin.

"I'm five-ten. Hundred forty." Emma thought how she probably shouldn't have told him that. It made her sound big and gross. Embarrassed, she grabbed a bale of hay and tossed it onto the bed, and then she was embarrassed again, for her easy throw probably made her look manly. She climbed onto the truck. "You bring 'em; I'll stack 'em." She hoped it sounded like she wasn't strong enough to manhandle them but that she would seem proficient enough to gain his appreciation.

In the dusk they worked, their young, struggling bodies giving them excuse for silence, a pretense that they would have things to say to each other if not for this task, a promise that there would be time for words. Just as the orange air shifted to purple, they finished. As Emma arranged the last bale, Holden handed her bike up. "I'll give you a ride."

"Oh, no," she said. "Please no."

"Okay," he said, lowering it back to the ground. He held the handlebars as if he were steadying one of their young horses as Emma threw her leg over the seat.

Smiling quickly at him, her teeth flashing a quick blue, "See ya," she said, and she pedaled away.

Waiting, Holden counted to twenty, feeling the air cool as the last bit of red left it, the purple going to dark blue. Then he started the truck and turned on the headlights, slowly moving ahead until the girl was framed in their yellow cast. He stayed behind her, protective, until she raised her arm and turned into her lane. He stopped the truck and gave the horn a light tap, enough to produce a bleat of goodbye, soft enough so it could not be heard at her house. He waited a minute, imagining her moving through the dark, up the lane to a world whose unfamiliarity enticed him, and then he slowly headed for his own house, imagining how he would explain to his father the unstacked hay.

During haying season, Emma was expected to be in the kitchen by 6:30, helping her mother get breakfast on the table and preparing some of the dishes for the noon supper. At 7:00, her dad and Tre would come down to eat. By 7:30, the men would be out the door, working on machinery as they waited for the night dew to burn off. By the time they finished changing out sickles or cleaning the baler or putting a new role of baling string in, Emma and her mother would have straightened the kitchen and gotten everything ready to go for the next meal. By 8:30, they'd all head to the fields with the equipment and a pickup. When they heard the engines turn over, Josey and Moby, their two border collies, would bound to their respective spots, Josey riding shotgun in the pickup, his wide, black muzzle smiling as he hung out the window, and Moby sitting spotted and clown-like on the lap of the tractor driver. And they would bark and bark at each other.

As she sat on her bed dressing at 5:00 and listening to the birds start to chip and warble and whistle, Emma worried what the dogs would do when she snuck out the kitchen door. Would they carry on because they thought she was off to the fields, or would they carry on because she was off schedule? Was it possible they would raise sleepy eyes to her and silently remain on their beds near the woodstove?

When she entered the kitchen, both heads came up and smiled and yawned and squeaked. "Shhh," she signaled to them, which only made them squeak louder and get up, wagging their tails and coming to her. "Shhh," she signaled again, more desperately, and they began to clack around in circles on the linoleum, growling at each other, grabbing each other's ruffs and play wrestling. "Shhh."

"Emma? Tre?" It was her mother's voice, coming from her parents' bedroom.

"Damn," she whispered as she headed upstairs, stopping in the threshold of their door. "It's me. I couldn't sleep. I thought I'd go look for bird nests. Be back by 6:30." Her father had had an egg collection he had smashed when his sister died. When Emma was born, he started all over again, taking her and then Tre, too, teaching them about habitat and nesting and mating patterns and eggs and birdlets and feathers and migration, helping them both keep journals of what they observed. Though Emma tried to be interested in eggs, it was the nests that moved her, those woven and plastered and designed and makeshift homes, so she became a collector. "You're just like your aunt," her father smilingly told her; "she didn't like eggs, either. She liked flight feathers." Because it was so important to her dad, Emma felt guilty lying to him this morning. But then, she thought, it was her right to have her own life; after all, she had been living part of his for seventeen years. Besides, they looked cozy, her mother closest to the door so that she could quickly get to any emergency in the house, her father curled around her back, both looking relaxed, both looking pleased by her early-morning ambition. Why should they impede her in her search for the same cozy future?

"Have fun." Her dad smiled as he dropped his head back to the pillow.

If the Awns were the same kind of family hers was, and she suspected they were, Holden would have met silence when he told his father he dumped the load, and that silence would let him know he had to get up early to unstack the hay so the pickup and trailer would be ready for another load. And if the stack was supposed to be in the river field, all she had to do was cut across her own family's meadow and then wade the river to be in his.

When she got to the edge of their land that looked down on the water, she paused. Though she knew the crossing, knew that her father and his sister and Holden's father and brothers and sisters used to go back and forth easily, she had never done so. She felt like an East Berliner she'd read about in her world history book, a person fleeing to the West, and she took a deep breath as she walked down the trail. At the water, she sat and took her shoes and socks off and rolled her pants up, and when she stepped in, Josey and Moby, who had followed her, barked at the new adventure, for they had never crossed, either.

As Emma emerged from the river, slivers of pink slipped through a crack in the sky onto a row of old cottonwoods, turning the leaves purple. She stopped to watch, and soon the sky opened like a door, and she was fully in the day, belonging to it, holding her own life, small and growing and fully illuminated.

In the new light was a figure atop a stack, arranging a row of bales. Behind him, up and down the staircase he had built, two dogs ran, pausing to bury their noses in the cracks between the bales, hallways for the mice. When they saw a figure and two dogs approaching, they stopped and then, running down the staircase, barked as they bounded toward the intruders. Unsure of themselves in new territory, Josey and Moby remained silent as they moved in front of Emma, the hair on their backs coming up, making their heads look sucked into their necks, and their legs moving stiffly, as if they walked on tiptoes.

Holden, turning at his dogs' alarm, saw who it was and felt powerful, for as he had lifted bales he thought of Emma; that she now walked toward him in this fresh light made him feel his thinking had made her so. Nevertheless, he did not move his eyes away from her, for if he did, she might disappear—she still seemed more imagination than reality.

The dogs had first walked broadly in circles around

each other, but now spiraled in, and by the time Emma reached the stack, they were all wagging tails as they sniffed each other's bottoms. "Can I come up?"

"Sure." He waited for her, watching her long legs easily climb the bales, chaff sticking to her wet pants. He had been on the stack since 5:00, hauling bales up the stairs to arrange the last layer, running them crosswise against the layer below so no moisture could drip farther down a crack than one level, and he was sweaty. But now, waiting in the new morning for her, he shivered.

"You must have got here early. The trailer's already half empty. I came to help."

"No need," he said, feeling full of need.

"I'll help you haul a bunch up here, then I'll stack." Happily they ran down the hay stairs together. Because he was stronger, for every bale she carried, he carried two. Excited, they hurried, and they could hear each other breathe heavily and grunt as they would pass. Once they had a dozen bales on top, Emma started carrying them across the thirty feet to the far end as Holden continued to move up and down. When he had them all hauled up, he stopped, winded, to watch how she moved. "No," he said, confused. "You don't stack that way, do you?" for she was not filling in the floor but instead making a wall one bale high around the perimeter. "More bales'll get wet this way."

"I'm making a nest," she explained. "It's only July. Before the rainy season, we'll fill it in."

Holden did not understand.

"For us. A nest for us." Emma's voice shook with the immensity of what she suggested. Certainly she was asking him to risk feed for the Awn cattle, more feed than a bad winter might allow. But more important, she was asking him to disobey the laws of their world, asking him to choose her over family, as she was choosing him, asking him to meet her often, hidden high in this house of grass.

She was still as Holden stood considering, and she felt her sweat begin to cool, giving her goose bumps. As he slowly grabbed a bale and carried it to the wall she had begun, Emma felt the points of her push against the world, her cold nose into the sky, her breasts against her T-shirt, her arms into the yellowing light. She watched her fingertips reach out to the full world and grasp what she wanted—the strings of a bale. She felt like a morning star.

2002

In the beginning was the deed.

HOW UNKIND the twilight, she thought, her chin resting on her hands, which steadied a shovel; how it forced one to finally measure a day, and the measurement had to be in loss—of light, color, warmth. Emma Orchard shivered, remembering that twilight was what her mother, when she was most drunk, claimed to miss the most about this place. "Tweenlight," she'd slur, or "twolight," or "twinlight."

"Double vision? Like a drunk?" Emma would ask to

vex her, for she had learned to speak of love, like twi-light, in measures of loss. Never in gain. Never.

"I don't know why you're so damned glum," her mother would complain, her words as blurry as Emma believed her memory to be. "Twilight is . . ."

How many times she had heard that incomplete ob-servation, her mother's voice trailing off, sometimes into a dreaminess, sometimes a sadness, sometimes a bitter-ness, always a numbness. No matter where they lived, what trailer or low-end house or basement apartment as they moved from Montana town to town, twilight would always come, reminding her mother, and she would leave that sentence hanging.

"Twilight is what, Mom? You need a nominative clause. Even though the verb *to be* is intransitive, your sentence doesn't sound finished."

But her mother would be staring into some place, some where, some time from which she was irretriev-able. So Emma would return to her books, which she believed would get her to some place, some where, some time she wanted to be—equally irretrievable.

Her mother, though, was stronger than Emma imag-ined. Or meaner, perhaps, for she co-opted Emma's dream of running away—by dying. "I beat you to it," she had whispered, her sick eyes wide in surprise that she was indeed leaving, that she could not stop it, and Emma's eyes wider that she would any second be totally alone, even though it was what she had longed for.

"I'm sorry," they said in unison, the last words spoken to one another.

Emma Orchard studied the two stones in the cemetery: EMMA ORCHARD, 1932 to 1949, and EMMA ORCHARD, 1958 to 2000. "No more Emma Orchards here," she said to the markers. She was not sure there should be two women of the same name in this place, two who for the third Emma Orchard reiterated a potentially bleak future. But her Uncle Tre had called, urging her to bring her mother back. "You don't want to lug those ashes around the rest of your life," he cajoled.

How odd, Emma thought, that she did. She was so unlike her mother in many ways—disciplined, college educated, employed. But she was also like her, always moving, looking for something, and so she'd poured the five pounds of uneven particles and bone fragments from the plastic box into an old leather suitcase, the one that had belonged to the first Emma and was gold embossed with an *E* and *O*, the one her mother had taken from the attic when she got pregnant and was kicked off the ranch. The luggage made it easy for the daughter to pack her mother in the car, and because her mother, despite her drunken inability to complete sentences, kept track of keys with the precision of an obsessive compulsive, Emma had locked her in the suitcase. Her mother would not leave her again, not until Emma was ready to relinquish her.

"You carry enough baggage around with you," Tre had joked. "She's been dead two years. It's time. And your grandpa's so senile he won't know the difference. Since he's at Mountain View Care Center, you can even come stay here now."

"What will the Awns say?" she'd wondered.

"I think they might be relieved it's all been put to rest. And if they aren't, who gives a horse's patooty?"

And so her kind uncle, who through the years had always kept track of his sister and her daughter, sending money when he could, visiting them when his sister was sober and would allow, had ordered a pink granite boulder, almost identical to the first, and placed it beside the other. Over the past two evenings, the two of them had dug a hole much larger and deeper than the suitcase needed. When it was finished, from the hole her uncle called, "Hand it down."

"I'll put her in," Emma said.

He passed the shovel up to her, then his arms appeared above the earth as if he were someone trying to escape it. "Help me out?"

Sitting on the edge of the grave, she had grasped his hands, loving the warm roughness of him, and leaned back as he scurried up the sides with his feet. Once on top, he scuffed his muddy boots on the dust and wiped his hands on the back of his Levi's. "You ready?" he asked.

She nodded.

Taking hold of her hands, he lowered her. Standing still, Emma looked at the edge of light, out of which sage and weeds grew. Under her feet, the soil felt damp, and then she could see in the dimness the tunnels of earthworms, going only they knew where in this subterranean world, and roots of sage amputated by the sharp shovel, their scars glowing. "Okay," she said to the sky, and soon a suitcase filled it, putting her in its shadow. She felt her chest constrict in claustrophobia as she reached for it.

"You okay?"

"Yeah. Just a minute. It's . . ." Her sentence remained incomplete as she lowered the suitcase to the ground and then shakily shoved a hand into her pocket, looking for a flashlight. Emma shined it on the E and O to be sure the suitcase was right side up—as if her mother still had a head and feet and a heart in their proper places. "Okay," she heard herself say too quickly and loudly, and when his hands came down, she clamored for them, desperate to be pulled into something as unkind as twilight.

"You got anything you want to say?" Tre asked once he had Emma out.

"I'll do the rest alone."

"I figured as much. But you got anything you want to say? You know, 'Ashes to ashes, dust to dust'? Those kinds of things?"

"I never even thought . . ." Emma shook her head.

"Your mom loved it here," Tre said. "It's good she's back. Buckle, Montana. The last best place." He sighed. "At least for the second Emma." He leaned over and kissed the crown of his niece's head.

She waited until she could no longer see the dust from the pickup on the county road. Then Emma took her first shovel of dirt and let it dribble slowly onto the suitcase, lightly so she wouldn't hear it. When the luggage was covered, she impatiently heaped earth upon earth, now wanting the land to work its will.

As she walked the road toward her uncle's farmhouse, she knew from her mother's stories that somewhere along it, on a July evening, her mother came to know Holden Awn. It was this road that led to a hayfield the Awns owned, a hayfield with a stack twenty feet high and a wall on top. More used to city than landscapes and television than reality, Emma imagined a penthouse, but her mother said no, no, it was more a lark's nest, built from the ground up and nothing more than piled grass, really . . . just squared up because humans were involved.

At night they would meet there, this young Emma, bright and steady like a star. Or so her uncle said. And her father.

In that nest, Emma imagined them both discovering in the desultory, dusty twilight of a summer that they each needed something, and so they decided to become adults. Both were astounded at how lovely such a state was, dizzy as they disappeared into it. Because she, too, had loved, Emma imagined them first pretending, their touches tentative and exploratory. But then their pretense slowly pulled them into the deed, before they had a chance to test all the new feelings inside. Perhaps because her name was Emma Orchard or perhaps because she was her mother's daughter or perhaps because she was a woman, Emma could imagine her mother, still a girl, opening to her father, recognizing what he wanted before he did, confused in her defense as he pushed through her softening hands. And then she let him loose and became a woman. And what did he find? If her mother was once as shining as Tre said she was, what Holden Awn must have found was that she was marvelous, and lying in her nest, so was he.

Because Emma was twenty-seven, had had three lovers, and was still a solitaire, she understood that love was not simple or kind. And yet walking down this road whose shoulders curved gently into hayfields which ran to cottonwoods which ran to the river which ran from the mountains, it seemed as if here, at least, love should have been easier. For the first time, she doubted her belief that love made victims. Maybe it was the opposite— that love was a victim of people and their stories. After all, would she be alone if stories had not maligned love? And what would have happened to the love between her mother and Holden if the Orchards and Awns had not intervened, influenced by that very first story? For when he found out that Emma was pregnant, Emmet sent his daughter off to Helena, to the Florence Crittendon Home, where she was to have her baby and give it away. "Why didn't she abort me? Then she could have kept her life," Emma had asked Tre.

"Your grandfather wanted that. But your mom was in love; she was sure Holden would come for her. And once the Awns said they wanted you aborted, your grandfather changed his mind, just to spite them."

"Has he ever wanted to meet me?"

"Who?"

"My grandfather."

"No."

"Holden?"

"I don't know."

"Why did she keep me? Love or spite?"

"You would know better than me," Tre answered, but Emma didn't.

When she got back to the house, her uncle was sitting at the kitchen table reading the *Buckle Argus*. The purple night spilled through the windows, pushing against the ceiling light, threatening to overwhelm it, for one of the two bulbs had burned out. As the gloom clotted and thickened, Emma heard the tails of Tristan and Isolde, Tre's two mutts, who were in the black shadow under the table, beat a welcome against the floor. "Where are your bulbs? I'll change that one for you. You'll wreck your eyes."

"Naw, don't worry about it. I see better in the dark, anyway."

She sat down, and the dogs came up, resting their muzzles on her lap, wanting to be touched. "How come you have two dogs?"

"Just the way it is. Plus, when I'm not here, they have each other."

"Are you lonely in this house, all by yourself?"

Squinting, he looked up. "Since your mom left I've been alone, even when I wasn't. I'm used to it."

"How come you didn't leave?"

"My folks. I was expected to stay. Emma was supposed to leave—under different circumstances, of course—and I was to run the ranch."

"Did you want to?"

"It just wasn't that easy."

"What?"

"Wanting."

"It should have been."

"Yup."

"Is this the same table the first Emma—"

"Yup."

"Why don't you get rid of it?"

"It's an antique." Tre smiled sadly at her. "Everyone

says they want antiques because of the stories they hold, even though they don't know what the stories are." He rapped on the wooden surface with his knuckles. "I know this table's story. I know how it ended, and I know what people did with that ending, and how their stories ended."

The rattling of the paper told Emma Tre was finished talking, and Emma watched him as he flipped a page, his eyes scanning the headlines. She said, "I'm going to get up early and walk the fields."

Lowering the paper, he studied her. "Your life. Tris and Izzy'll go with you. Watch out for snakes."

"Night."

"Yup."

AS SHE WALKED through the newly mowed fields, Emma wondered why dawn wasn't called twilight, too, for it had the same in-between colors and shades and shadows, the same half-and-half feel of the evening. Perhaps it was because the morning was headed to completion rather than depletion; there was a cadence rather than a decadence of light. And in such light, double vision was impossible, except in the disillusioned. How kind the dawn, she thought. Or misleading.

She tried to climb a bale to feel what her mother might have, but she couldn't; it was huge—at least six feet in diameter; and it was round; and it was slippery, for it was wrapped in plastic. The plastic kept all moisture out, so there was no need to stack. Rather, the bales were lined up in a row. Because each weighed several hundred pounds, Tre used a hydraulic pin on the back of his pickup to lift them. Like a spindle it would go through the center of the hay spool and, when he was ready to feed, the hay would unroll like a green-and-blue Persian rug—a long, colorful runner sprinkled with blue alfalfa blossoms in a monochromatic winter room in which the cattle lived. She thought of the two Emmas after whom she'd been named and how stacked hay had been the downfall of both. "Probably better," she said to the empty world as she stared at the unstacked and unassailable spool of grass. "Death control. Birth control."

Walking along the meadow's edge, Emma looked down on the river, wondering where the crossing was. It was a place that should have been destroyed, for look what crossing over had done to two generations of family. When she saw it, though, she understood how impossible that would be, for the land would work its will. While much of the bank was steep, at the crossing it gentled and sloped easily down, a safe passage to water and feed for wildlife and livestock, a safe passage for all but Orchard girls.

Because of its easy invitation to the river, which in the cascading light sparkled, Emma accepted. It was an intuitive and spontaneous acceptance, and she knew it, and it frightened her. As she followed the trail, she heard above her a yip and then another one; Tris and Izzy, who had been so busy mousing in the meadow that they'd paid her no heed, had looked up to find her gone. Following their noses, though, they now looked down upon her and barked. Emma stopped, trying to understand what they said: go no farther, they perhaps warned, canine Horatios at the gate. But when they tumbled by her, crashing into each other, she knew they were pleased. Either that, or they were very bad guard dogs. At water's edge, she sat down on the cobblestones to remove her shoes and socks.

"COME HERE," Holden Awn said to Romy and Remus. The two Australian shepherds, born to work but still young enough to play, came up to him. Romy was grinning with gratitude, his canines yellow in the lemon light of morning as he was lifted onto the tall round bale, and Remus waited patiently, his docked tail vibrating, to be set next to his littermate. When he had both his dogs up, Holden, born to work but still young enough to play, balled a fist and jammed it into the end of the bale, into the swirls of hay, like a climber would into a rock fissure, feeling the coarse, dried stems of timothy and alfalfa scratch and slice his knuckles and the back of his hand. At the same time, he drove his toe into the grass. Now he could swing his other hand onto the top of the spool and leverage himself up. As he did, the dogs silently nibbled at the top of his head, his neck, the back of his shirt, tickling him and then barking as he laughed. He rolled onto his back and lay still for a moment, looking up at the sky still softened by night, still dim enough that he did not have to squint. His quiet calmed the dogs, and they sat down next to him. Their breeding would not let them study the sky and so they scanned the land.

Sitting up, Holden stared with the dogs into the west, where the distant faces of the mountains gathered the first light and the canyons hid from it. The whole stretch of range was one of simple geometry—triangles of pink and lines of purple and angles of black—and it was all figured on a tablet of sky whose shades shifted steadily but imperceptibly from blue to pink to yellow. Every dawn, Holden thought, the sky was like springtime, when you wait and wait for the leaves, and the buds get bigger and bigger and the green starts to squeeze out, and you're sure you'll see winter trees turn to summertime ones . . . and you miss it, just like he would not see this day come, even while he waited and watched. No, he would feel it more than see it, for when the sun finally popped over the ridge behind him, the atoms of the air would warm and expand, making a breeze that he would feel upon his back, and the grass he and his father had mowed just yesterday in the east half of the field would still be moist, and as the wet warmed and seeped from the cut timothy, the smell of green would wash over him. He would miss this, he thought, as he put an arm around each of his dogs—this part of his life, the feel of it all.

But his mother had told him there was more to feel than Montana, and there was more to think than feel. "Come out to Washington for your last year of high school," she'd urged; "live with me, get your residency, and go to college. Try wet rather than dry agriculture," she'd teased him over the phone. She couldn't see that the seep of grass was enough for him. When he tried to explain, her teasing stopped. "You need to be away from your dad."

"Who says?" he'd challenged.

"I do."

"He's doing all right."

"Holden, he isn't."

And, as usual, their conversation ended in a kind of double vision, him saying that his dad didn't talk at him like he had, that he didn't talk at all, and that was fine, he could handle the quiet; and his mom saying that he deserved more than silence. "But the ranch . . . ," he'd quietly offered, knowing that while his mom had quit loving his dad, she loved the place he'd first brought her to.

"It will be there for you later," she said. "Come work with apples rather than grass and cattle."

"No, it won't. I'll go, then Grandpa'll die, and there'll be no one to make him work it. He'll sell it. It'll get subdivided."

"So be it," she'd said.

"No."

And then she told him he was still a minor and she had custody of him and had only let him stay because he wanted to, but it wasn't working and he knew it, and if he didn't come, she and her father would be back in court to finalize the divorce, at which point the ranch would have to be sold. If he came now, maybe his dad would hold onto it long enough for him. It was one long run-on sentence with all the answers, like she'd been writing and rewriting it and rehearsing and practicing. It made him smile to think of her trying so hard for him. "And Romy and Remus can come," she'd finished up.

"They'll love working apples," he complained.

"If they stay, he'll run 'em off," his mother countered.

She was right. It was the admission that his father couldn't even love the dogs that convinced Holden. And so he was going, once haying season was over. When he told his dad, his father just looked at him and walked out of the kitchen.

His mom said that was the problem—he always let everybody do what they wanted, and he never did what he wanted, and he never said what he wanted, and it all made him angry. "He shouldn't have married me."

"Did you want to marry him?"

"Yes. But he didn't want to marry me. His dad told him what to do. He was still in love with another girl."

Even though his mother had become the neighbor to this girl's family, she never named her. "Emma Orchard," Holden said.

"Yes."

Because he was just seventeen, Holden didn't wonder what his dad was like when he was his age; instead, he wondered what he would have been like if he'd been born to his dad and Emma Orchard. He had looked at their pictures in the high school yearbook, and, except for her hairdo, she was pretty, looking a little like his mom. Holden thought he himself was handsome, but he wondered what he'd be like if he'd grown up with whole parents, rather than one-and-a-half. He wondered what he'd be like if he'd been able to grow up happy.

WHEN SHE CAME through the cottonwoods, Emma slowed, taking in the whole scene—the hayed meadow, the grass spools proving its fertility, windrows waiting to be gathered, the August sky flaring in the morning breeze, and a man and two dogs on top of a bale. It had to be an Awn. She turned to disappear into the purple of the cottonwoods, but his dogs spotted her and, jumping off the bale, came rushing and barking. The man stood and, seeing a figure, slid down the side of the bale, watching.

"Romy, Remus, you get back here now!" Holden shouted, for the figure was a woman, and she came from the direction of the Orchard place. It had to be the daughter. It had to be Emma. They had heard she was around, and his dad was scarcer than usual. "Romy! Remus!"

The dogs would not heed him. They thought they were doing their job. "Shit," he said under his breath. What was he supposed to do?

And so they both stared at each other, he in the sun of a new day, she in its shadow, twilight figures, half brother and half sister.

The four dogs met partway through the meadow, and they found no reason to fight, and so the two people held still.

"Holden," Emma whispered, in recognition of his familiarity to her. She raised her hand.

It was an austere but colorful world where nothing seemed out of place, nothing to make Holden Awn think he was any different than the night before, nothing to make him think he was any different, nothing except Emma. He raised his hand and waved back.

Horse Thieves

A BIRTH IS FULL OF MAGIC. IT'S LIKE THE EMPTY BOX THE magician closes up, taps with his wand, and spins round and round. When the spinning stops and he opens it, out comes something that wasn't there before—a beautiful lady or tiger or dove, and all of a sudden you realize that you were waiting, knowing the space would be filled just right. The magic's in the just-right part.

But there's also a smaller part of the magic I like as much. It's when the new baby takes something for the very first time from the world, and nothing's telling it to, but everything is. It's that first stolen breath, a big, startled one, the biggest one ever because the baby's lungs have never had anything in them before. Nothing at all. After that, all the other breaths will be married up in pairs of in and out, except the last one where the body comes full circle and gives back what it took when it was born, and nothing's telling it to, but everything is. And that last breath out is magic like the first breath in. The show reverses itself, and the space that was filled with something big is emptied out again. Poof . . . all gone.

You probably think I'm talking about human babies, but I'm not. While I know the magic is there with them—it's there with rats, too—humans are wrinkled and splotchy with squinty faded eyes when they're born. They're not like horses, which are what I'm talking about. Unlike a human, a foal comes out perfect and ready for life, with its coat wet and its eyes open, standing up quick to the world once it gets its nose out of that birthing sac and steals the first breath. And that breath is big, so much bigger than one a human takes. What's more, a horse seems important because of the amount of space it takes up. I suppose an elephant baby would seem even more important, but I've never seen one of them born. And they aren't nearly as pretty in form as a little foal.

There's something else that makes horses more magical. Other babies get born almost anytime. But most mares foal in the night, when the sky's all blued with stars and the world's all hushed up, almost as if it's waiting for the new little creature. And you are waiting, too, and expectant. You've been watching that mare for clues—a certain standoffishness that comes with the waxing up of her teats, almost like she's putting lids on two milk bottles. And if you want, and if the mare's in a stall, you wait with her in the dark blue world for the magic to come.

Sometime in that waiting night, you drift off because you're tired from doing chores all day, and the straw you've put out for the mare and yourself smells like sunshine and summer dust. While you sit in your little grassy mound of gold, your eyelids drop with every falling star.

What wakes you is the sound of running water, not the sound of pissing, which sounds like a water drill boring into the earth, but a more general splashing sound, like birds in a bath. Your eyes pop open and then you squint, a blind person in the night waiting for the magic because the mare's water has broken.

Finally you see her outline, and she is standing above the straw bed you've made for her so when her foal drops, she'll land soft in the space that has been waiting for her. If the mare was out in the pasture, she would let the baby drop to the hard earth, but, like all of us should do, she'll give comfort when and where she can.

You have to sit quiet while you wait so she doesn't move away from the soft bed you've offered her. Soon, from beneath her tail, which she holds slightly up, a hoof appears, and then another. They look like a present in the heavy, shiny wrapping of the placenta, and you feel like you're getting a gift and you know what it is because you can see its outline. You try to pretend, though, that you don't know because you don't want to jinx the birth.

The hooves are soft because they've been floating in liquid for almost a year, but they're sharp enough so that if all goes like the magician planned, their edges will slice the wrapping just as the foal's muzzle appears between those two hooves. In the shadow of the mare, it will be hard to see the nostrils, but they are there; they're not taking in air yet because the baby's chest is pressed tight in the birth canal, and the lungs can't push out. This is magic, too, because if the hooves haven't torn the wrapping of the sac yet, then there's no need to breathe. All the baby would do is breathe in the fluids of her own making, suck herself up and die. And so, with her mother's help of throbbing muscles, she slowly wiggles from her world of not quite being into yours of night and stars and straw and earth. The hooves and head drop downward, but the body still resists. If the hooves haven't already done their job, the opposite pullings of gravity and resistance will rip the sac, and the foal slips into life.

The mother turns and gives a soft rumbling in her chest and nose, both welcome and relief, as she bends to lick her baby clean. Then you can clearly see the magic. Even though nothing is telling her to, everything is, and the foal's ribs float outward as she steals her first breath from the world. She is like a thief in the night, and you have come to love a thief.

Of my heartful of horse thieves, I loved Jasmine the best. Her name was Al Mouad al Sahid al Fayedah al Jasmine. You can probably tell from the name that she was an Arabian, and her name traced her story, which was as complicated as anything out of Arabian Nights. Her great-grandfather was Fayed, her grandfather Sahid, and her dam Fayedah, the daughter of Sahid. Both Mouad and Sahid were black stallions, and Fayedah's dam, Jasmine's grandmother, had been black, too.

Fayedah, or Fay, as I called her, like most of the Arabian breed, was born black but within two years had faded to a dappled gray. Nevertheless, her genes made it quite possible for her to throw a black foal, and so her lot in life was cast. She was a broodmare; every two to three years, in late spring, her marriage to a black stallion in Nevada or California or Oregon was arranged. She'd get shipped out, and two months later she'd come home, a little thinner and pregnant. Through the winter I would tend to her to make sure the magic would happen again.

To me, magic happened no matter the color of the foal, but to the lady I worked for, magic would come when a foal spun out black. So far, that hadn't happened. Before I came to work, Fay had had three babies. One was a bay, and two had been born black but had the tell-tale signs of turning gray or white—a few white hairs scattered throughout their coats. Sure enough, one was a pretty little dapple like Fay and the other was an ugly scuffed white.

When Jasmine stole into my world that night, I could tell she was dark, but that was all. And I didn't have a flashlight because that would have made me some kind of Peeping Tom, separated from the magic, watching rather than being a part of it. I'm not sure all these mechanical gadgets we have are that big a help to us, not when they cut us off. So I watched by what little light the night gave me, which was enough, as Fay licked her baby. And then I fell asleep. I tell you now that I did not see Jasmine get up. I did not.

"What have we got?"

That was Wendy. Her voice had the qualities of an alarm clock. Oh, her tones were soft enough; she was from back East and had gone to good schools, and she knew how to talk good. But there was always something pushy and grating, and I think it had to do with money. Her voice had the sound of coins, kind of tinkly, like pennies in a china pig. She sounded like a bank, and people with money who wanted horses—mind you, they didn't love them but they wanted them—were attracted to her voice and without a flinch would deposit $10,000 in her. And then would her voice jingle!

I came up from underneath my straw mound, startled like a mouse, and there she was glowing in the orange light of daybreak. In June that meant it was only 5:30, and I rubbed the broken bits of last year's wheat stalks out of my eyes. She was kneeling over the little horse, who in my blurry vision looked black. I couldn't tell by my own eyesight if there were white hairs in the baby's coat anywhere, but Wendy's voice sounded like the U.S. Mint, so I figured she'd finally got herself a black Arabian.

Despite her voice, though, something didn't seem right, so as I combed the straw out of my snarled hair with my fingers, I thought on it. If the horse was dead, then Wendy's voice wouldn't be full of milk and money. But why would I think the little horse was dead? Then I jumped up in a hurry. "Why isn't it standing up?" I asked as I moved toward Wendy. "It was born a while ago. What is it?"

"A filly," Wendy answered. And then she announced her name like the horse was some kind of princess. "Al Mouad al Sahid al Fayedah al Jasmine." She'd been saving that family tree handle for the black horse she kept telling herself and the bank she'd get some day.

"No, not that. What is it that's making her stay down?"

When I got up to the straw bed, there rested the prettiest little ink horse you'd ever want to see, a horse as dark and shiny as a moonless night, and I liked her right away, for her appearance had the qualities of the night she stole into. My eyes ran over her resting form, her hind legs tucked underneath her and to the side, as girl-ish as could be, her front legs out straight and relaxed, like a resting ballerina's. Her head was refined, for Fay was an Egyptian Arabian, the side of the family known for their spooned-out noses, but her father was from the Anglo side, whose muzzles were straighter and larger. Her head was a good genetic nick, then, with a soft gen-tle curve to the profile. "You are perfect, aren't you?" I whispered, and I glanced at the dried strand of umbilical cord lying stiffly out from her belly, the only proof that she was conceived in the normal way rather than in a magician's head.

She just stared at us with eyes that didn't know distrust yet. There was nothing but a chocolate wonder to them.

I looked at Wendy, whose own eyes were filled with dollar signs. "She should be up and nursing, not just sit-ting here," I said. "Let's help her up."

When we lifted her, the hind legs didn't unfold like liquid, like they should. Instead, they dropped only a lit-tle ways, all dry and stiff. When I bent down to see why, I saw her hocks. They were swollen like the big knuck-lebones of a grownup cow.

"Holy . . ."

"What?" Wendy's voice snapped, and the money drained out of it as she bent to see what I was seeing. For a $4,000 stud fee, Wendy might have finally gotten herself a black mare, but the mare was going to need a wheelchair. A black horse in a wheelchair is hard to breed. And a black horse that goes unbred doesn't pay her board.

Wendy let go of her side, and little Jasmine started to crumple. I hurried up and cradled her butt to keep her from falling. "Where you going?" I asked Wendy's retreating form.

"To call the goddamned vet."

Gently I lowered the little baby to her bed and then went to the barn to grab a bucket and a large baby bottle. I knelt next to Fay and began to strip her teats of the first milk that Jasmine should have already had. It was the colostrum that would make a baby strong. I poured the liquid into the king-sized bottle and attached a latex nipple, and the smell of that rubber made me so sad. Jasmine should have been under her mother, smelling that rich smell of horse, of hair and sweat and grass and milk. Rubber was not the first taste of life Jasmine—or for that matter, any new creature—should have.

When I knelt down in front of her, though, the little indigo made it plain she didn't care what life tasted like. She just wanted it. Her black-pencil lips opened, and she bit the latex nipple, her sweet, pink, toothless but bony gums grabbing hold like a snapping turtle and not letting go. When it was empty, I had to yank it out of her mouth. I hurried to pour more colostrum into it, and Jasmine tried to follow me, struggling to get up and get up and get up, and falling and falling and falling. "Stay still," I kept pleading with her, but she wouldn't till I came back and she grabbed hold of that nipple again. For five bottles we did that, and by the time we had finished, I knew two things. That little crippled and hungry horse figured I was her mother. And I figured I was her mother. That morning feeding is how I came to love her more than any other horse I'd ever seen born. And like a mother, I didn't care if she wasn't perfect. She was to me. She was mine.

The only problem was she wasn't. I found that out a few hours later when Doc McTee, the vet from Buckle, showed up.

Wendy stood impatiently apart, her arms folded across her chest and her fingers tapping like runaway horses while I struggled to hold Jasmine up and the man who looked more like a cowboy than a doctor ran his big broken hands over her hocks and hummed. He rubbed and he hummed, and he hummed and he rubbed, and I could feel the sweat drip through my messy hair and soak my shirt and make me itch all over from the straw chaff. I looked pleadingly at Wendy to help me with the hundred pounds of horseflesh, but she wouldn't get near Jasmine. I could tell she thought she'd been defrauded.

The humming stopped and McTee stood up. "The stud was too big."

"It's the stud's fault?" Wendy snapped, her fingers still tapping away.

"I didn't say that. I said the stud was too big. How tall was he?"

"Oh, I don't know. Sixteen-two."

He pointed at Fay. "Fay here's only fourteen, I'd say." Then he pointed at Jasmine. "This foal didn't have enough room. As she grew, her legs were forced tighter and tighter into her body, and she couldn't move 'em."

He pointed at her hocks. "Her tendons are underdeveloped, and the joints are probably fused."

"What do I do now?"

McTee shrugged.

"Will she get better?"

He shrugged again.

Wendy stood in the noon light. The sun was straight up, so she cast no shadow, almost like she didn't exist. Or at least like she wasn't human. And what she said next made me know that was true. "Kill her," she said.

McTee shrugged.

"No." That's what I told her. No. "I'll take care of her."

Wendy just looked at me, a surprised grimace on her face. "And just how are you going to do that?"

It was my turn to shrug, for I had no idea. Where I labored was where I lived. I had no money, and I had no place, and I'd never felt more powerless. There Wendy stood, looking past McTee and at me, and I could tell by her face what she saw. I was all hunched over and sweaty, my hair all askew and full of straw, holding a crippled horse like she was my baby, the hired help who slept outside with pregnant mares because I believed in magic. What she saw was an idiot.

I looked at McTee, and I could tell he saw the same thing.

The difference between Wendy and McTee, though, is when Wendy sees an idiot, she gets all huffy and superior. When McTee sees one, he gets sorry. And so what McTee did next saved my pride and saved little Jasmine.

"Exercise and hot and cold packs might work." He

just kept looking at me. "Maybe those joints aren't fused. Maybe they're just inflamed. If we could get the swelling down and get her moving, those tendons and ligaments would stretch out . . ."

"Well, then, why don't we just take X-rays to see? If they're fused, I won't waste my time. And if they're just inflamed, why not use steroids?"

"No need to do either of those just yet," McTee said.

"Why not?"

"Steroids are unhealthy for everyone, let alone a foal. And they're expensive. Real expensive. Hot and cold packs are cheap. And no need to spend money on the X-rays. We'll know in a couple of weeks if it works." He turned from me and faced Wendy. "Look, you've got a lot invested in this little horse, and you've got the hired hand to tend her. Give it a try. It'll cost you some hot water and rags. The rest of the time'll come off her back." He tipped his head toward me.

I knew what McTee was doing. He was appealing to Wendy's stinginess. And he didn't want X-rays used because the X-rays would show there was no point, that her hired help's time could be better spent dunging out stalls.

It's always seemed to me that I'm not very smart. But that day with old Doc McTee I saw I wasn't as bad off as Wendy, for she let him talk her out of killing Jasmine. "All right," she said. "She can do it." That day I realized she didn't have God or brains or anything else on her side. She just had money. I also realized that she and folks like her would always have it. This was because her actions were always tied to money. Folks like me, though, would always be poor. This was because our actions were always tied to magic. We believed that things would turn out just because they should. That afternoon, when I was done with all my chores, I dunged out two stalls in the barn. Into one I moved my sleeping bag and a comb, and into the other I moved Fayedah and Jasmine. Starting that night and going on through the following weeks, I would pack her hocks and find a way to exercise her. It would work because it should.

"WINDY OUGHTN'T order me about," Rory said. "I'm no hired man; I'm her lover. I'll take the front end; you take the back." Rory put the frayed halter on the perfect head, and he pulled while I lifted. "She don't 'preciate me atall, all I do to make her feel good. No self-spectin' man'd put up with her horseshit." He tugged on the head while I carried the hind end. "She's frigid to boot. Did you know that? You're lettin' that side droop. Lift up more."

While I could pack Jasmine's legs by myself, I couldn't hold her up and move her around, so the next day I told Wendy I needed help. Notice that I say "told" rather than "asked." This is because McTee had evened the playing field; I didn't feel nearly so puny next to Wendy anymore. And there was a need beyond just saving Jasmine. It was my belief in magic against hers in money.

So when I told Wendy I needed help, she sent Rory, her other hired hand. Even though Rory and I had the same work title, there were a few differences. First, he was dumber. Second, he was better looking. Third, he had a penis. The second and third reasons put him in

Wendy's graces or something, and while he didn't move into the big house, he slept many a night there. Even though he was never invited to her dinner parties—she didn't want him to talk to anybody—Rory didn't think he should have to work in anything as low as the barn, but, nevertheless, Wendy had sent him to help with Blackie. That was the new name she had bestowed on Jasmine because of her hocks. Just as there was no reason to spend money on X-rays, there was no reason to waste a princess name on a cripple. She referred to her like some stray dog. Only I still called her Jasmine.

Every morning Rory and I did this, him walking in circles for a half an hour pulling on the lead while I carried the tail end of the little horse that dragged two furrows in the earth with her useless legs. Each day I became less sure of my belief, thinking that maybe I should not imagine anything—just see the overwhelming world around me: the sky was blue, just blue, and the ground was green, *green*, and there were all kinds of lines that ran between the blue and green and there was water that went across the land, fat and flush. And that was all there was. Why was I clinging to the notion that the land and the creatures on it made magic, when every day Wendy seemed to prove that what the land and the creatures on it were really meant to do was make money?

Then, well into the second week, something happened. I was holding Jasmine up as usual, feeling the dusty drag of her legs, when all of a sudden there was a bump in the drag. I thought she'd hit a rock in the earth, and I kept holding her, but there it was again, a bump. I looked down, watching her hooves plow the earth, and as I watched, one lifted up and then set down. A step. I interrupted one of Rory's monologues. "Rory, look at this." As he pulled on the halter, he watched the earth, and he saw it, too—drag and a bump.

"Windy; hey, Windy! Windy, looksee this, Windy! Looksee Blackie!" He dropped the lead and went screaming out of the barn to get his keeper. I understood his motives, and I didn't begrudge him. Life in her bed, though probably unpleasant, was better than life on some grub line. Once, I suspected, we had been alike in our beliefs. But while mine had waned, they hadn't totally disappeared. Rory's had. He now believed in Wendy and her way, and if he could he would take credit for Blackie's resurrection.

As I stood there holding Jasmine's hind end up, I worried that such weak trust in my world would hurt the little horse, so gently I released her and waited for her to fold down to the ground. Instead, she stood wobbling there on her own.

"Jasmine, Jasmine?" It was Wendy, and she and Rory came running through the door. "Jasmine's walking?"

I grinned at her use of the princess name even as I grimaced. For it meant that magic was afoot, and because of it I would lose my little horse. I would have lost her anyway. Once again, I felt puny next to Wendy. All my work, which had looked crazy and stupid to everyone, had just turned smart and sassy in Wendy's world—the world I didn't belong to. Magic would save Jasmine but rob me.

After that morning, Wendy began to boss me around about how to care for Jasmine. Now Rory and I had two big exercise programs a day, and with each day the little indigo horse wobbled less and walked more. With each night's packing, the swelling in her hocks lessened. All of this brought on the day I was dreading. "Put Jazz and Fay out in the small pasture," Wendy ordered. "With the extra time you can begin halter breaking the other foals." That afternoon, I let her and Fay go through the gate to the biggest world she had ever been in, and I moved my sleeping bag and comb back to my little house.

The next morning, we rounded up one of Wendy's mares and her little colt, slipping a halter on the dam and walking across the ranch compound to the indoor arena. Where the mare went, the foal was sure to follow. As I led them through the bright sunlight, I glanced at Fay and Jasmine, who were grazing out farther and farther, and I watched their shiny bodies, knowing that every step by Jasmine was one more away from me. Then I took the mare and colt through the sliding doors and shut them. As soon as the dam and foal and I got used to the dark coolness, Rory distracted the mare with grain while I slipped the halter on her baby boy. There were a few moments of fighting, but when he saw his mother could care less, he resigned himself to his newest mark of tameness. We led him around in the arena for half an hour and then freed him. The next day we would do the same, and it depressed me how this little colt would never learn to like us but would learn to put up with us.

There were a dozen new foals that summer, and we had them all pretty well started when Wendy said it was time to get working with Jasmine again, who had done nothing for a few weeks but get strong.

It's a funny thing about stories. Sometimes when you want to tell them, you don't know what the words should be. So you throw a rope out into a whole herd of possibilities, hoping to catch anything, and you snag just the right one by a hind foot, and then another by a front. Your catching is awkward, but you drag them in and all of a sudden you've got a nice little string, and you sit back and admire your catching. That's how I feel when I tell you that the day I started working with Jasmine as a real horse, not a cripple, was just plain blue. Just plain blue.

That was the sky in the morning. It had nothing in it but blue, and that color went every which way. Like the sky, things looked simple. I went to the holding pasture to catch Fay, and she came up to me, with Jasmine right next to her. But Jasmine, little Jasmine, when she saw me slip the halter on her mama, she took off. The grass was all twinkly with dew, and her hind legs, which were never supposed to work, threw a train of sparkles onto my face, like they were magic. She was so pretty to watch. She didn't have a regular gait yet because her hocks were still puffy, so her hind legs came down together, making her look like a little rocking horse. She rocked through all that blue tossing her head and shimmying her sides, just glad to be alive, and I was glad for her. When she was done showing off, she came close to Fay but not to me, which kind of hurt my feelings, and followed her across to the arena.

When I slid the door shut behind them, Rory came out with a grain pan. While Fay ate, I slipped the halter up over Jasmine's muzzle, buckled it, attached the lead, and wrapped the end of it around my hand. You never do that with a horse because you don't want to be too strongly attached. But Jasmine wasn't just a horse. She was my horse. Or so I thought.

She took off; a black bundle of muscles and nerves bounding across that arena with me on the end of the lead, trying to get it unwrapped. I felt like a big fish that had just been hooked. During one of the fastest dashes anybody's ever run in cowboy boots, I looked up and knew what my future was. It was corrugated and made of tin. I closed my eyes and could see my shape pushed into that wall about two feet above the ground like some cartoon character's.

Then I remember looking at the tin, but my shape wasn't there so I wasn't sure if I'd hit it. I was lying in the dirt with chunks of dry horse manure in my hair and face and all over my shirt. I looked around for Jasmine, but she was nowhere to be seen. Neither was Fay. Or Rory. It made me think that maybe I'd gone to Buckle and gotten drunk and come back and passed out in the arena, and now I was waking up. I started moving all my parts around, and everything worked except my left ankle. I was relieved, because that was the proof I'd hit the wall rather than the bottle. "Rory?" I called.

Nothing.

"Rory?"

The door, which was opened slightly, let in a slat of that plain blue which colored the dangling dust. I put my head down in the soft, fertilized dirt and just watched, enjoying the brightness and lightness, and then a shadow blocked it. "Rory?"

He broke through the blue and bent over me on his tippy-toes. Then he just stared.

"Why'd you run off?"

How he whined. "Why'd you do this to me? You know how Windy feels 'bout Jasmine. You coulda kilt that horse!"

"Rory. Shut up." I came out of the dust feeling like Eve must have when she was first made—small and bent, not quite put together, barely more than a rib bone. "I think my ankle's broken. Go get Wendy. Tell her Jasmine threw me against the barn."

"I can't tell her that. You know how she feels 'bout horses."

"Okay, okay. Tell her I threw myself against the barn. Just leave Jasmine out."

He ran off. Real fast Wendy was there. "Where's Jasmine? Is she all right?"

"Yup, I put her and Fay back in the pasture," Rory bragged as he tried to help me up.

Then she turned her attention to me. "What did you do?"

I tested my ankle, feeling the bone push against my skin like some trapped animal that wanted out. I had a feeling if I told her Jasmine had thrown me into the wall, she'd fire me on the spot. So I shrugged. "I don't know. I hit the barn wall. My ankle's broke. It's broke bad."

I looked into her face, her eyes, and they were just plain blue. She had no loyalty to me, I could see it. I was livestock, bought cheap and paid for. Unlike Jasmine, I had no kind of return. I was just some fool who on any day might throw herself into tin walls, so I deserved to lose my job.

Which I did. She cut me loose on the spot, giving me $500, her promise to pay my medical expenses, and Rory, but just to take me in to the hospital.

I sat in her brand-new Jeep while Rory went to the little house and threw my belongings into my duffel bags. While he was gone, I stared out the window at the holding pasture, where Fay and Jasmine grazed. I watched Jasmine's pretty little muzzle nibble at the grass. She looked up once at the car, and then she went to Fay and impatiently threw her head under her belly for milk. I had to smile at how horsey she'd become, and how spoiled. I watched her for as long as I could while Rory drove down the lane and out. That day made me just plain blue.

ABOUT A YEAR LATER, I ran into Rory in the Trout Creek Bar. He told me that after a decade, Wendy had tired of the horse-breeding business and was selling out, planning on going back East.

"It's okay," Rory said about losing his job. "She said it was no place for me."

Poor Rory. I know what she probably said was he had no place in her next world, made up of buildings and art and culture and money. In that unhorsey place, she'd need a different kind of stud than him.

"Where'd Jasmine go?" I asked.

"California. Broodmare. Windy got twenty-two thousand for her."

"What'd you get?"

"I got me another ranch job." He grinned. "It's okay."

I got me another job, too, but not on a ranch. I work in a nursing home now as a certified nurse's aide, emptying bedpans and rotating patients in their beds and bathing them and combing their hair and helping them walk down the halls. Sometimes when I lift their weak old haunches it reminds me of Jasmine and how I lifted her weak new ones. I don't quite get why I need a certificate for my job, other than I'm certified nuts to put up with it.

I guess, though, if truth be told, there's another reason besides being crazy. On a day, I'll go into some box stall of a room, and there's a body in there that's coming full circle, giving back what it took when it was born, and nothing's telling it to, but everything is. And that last breath out is magic like the first breath in. The show reverses itself, and the space that was filled with something beautiful is emptied out again. Poof . . . all gone.

Late Evening, June 14

AT THE STATION WHERE THE NIGHT NURSE DOZED, RAG THE cat tried to make a bed. First he climbed onto the nurse's lap to burrow into the wide *V* of her crotch, but she pushed him off when he started to paw her green polyester pants, his nails pushing through the fabric. Twice, as soon as her head nodded and bobbed, he returned with a silent, graceful leap to knead her doughy legs, and twice she swept him to the floor. Finally, he curled into the circular bed the staff provided when they'd let him in that day of the blizzard, his ears and tail frostbitten and his bad eye crusted shut. The nurses snipped away the dead tissue of his ears as needed so that the both of them now looked like furry shells with curled, zigzag edges; and the whole staff chipped in so that Doc McTee, the vet, would remove the tip of his frozen tail, sew up the eye with the shriveled ball, and castrate him. In the weeks they nursed him back to health, the staff had named him Rag because all his edges were so tattered.

Now all he ever wanted was coziness, and his bed, pressed against a cool metal file cabinet and exposed to the bald fluorescent light, was not that. In a tight ball, his shortened tail barely covering an ear, Rag looked indifferently out with his one yellow eye. The station and hall beyond, reflecting a vacant white of constant daytime, belied night. The wards of the Buckle Retirement and Nursing Care Facility slept, either on their own or with the help of Lorazepam stirred into their pudding; and the nurse snoozed over an article in a women's magazine: "New Uses for Old Things."

Rag pushed his front legs out and flexed his tufted orange knuckles, the claws extending and then retracting in the faux sheepskin of his bed. He raised himself and arched his back, his chopped tail twisting to the left, and then leaped onto the counter of the station, where he stared at the nurse for a long time, nothing but the ends of his whiskers quivering.

Slowly he stretched a paw forward to push at a yellow pencil. At first, it hardly moved, so he stiffened his leg to roll it across the counter and onto the floor. With its landing, Rag jumped down and on pigeon toes walked to the glass door to look upon the outside world from which he had come.

A full moon blued the single-storied buildings that huddled on the south end of Buckle; it coated the handles of the pumps at Harold's Stop N'Go gas station, flecked the picture window of the Buckle River Café, and ran down the wide western street in a slow, clear current, lapping over the few cars and pickups left overnight, and finally pooling around the tall cottonwoods of the city park.

Rag studied the scene. He was a middle-aged cat who had always lived in the old sheds and barns scattered around the small town, and though now sealed in the world of the care facility with its own smells of mop buckets and urine and feces and disinfectant and laundry and kitchen steam, he sometimes dreamed the fragrance of a summer night—the clarity of dew drops on cottonwood leaves, the astringency of moist darkness on sagebrush, the fishiness of the Buckle River, the muskiness of mouse fur and the rustiness of blood. And he dreamed the sounds, as well: the pebbles of sand tumbling under his paw pads as he walked, the talons of barn swallows scratching the mud of their nests, the soft unrolling of rhubarb leaves, the tapping of a flicker's beak on box elder bark, the muffled tunneling of worms, the moth's wing beat just before he snagged it from the air; he dreamed the whole roar of life that lay on the other side of the glass door as he stood in the silence of the side he now inhabited.

Rag was not nostalgic for any of this. Here, where the bland taste of kibble was daily provided and on occasion punctuated with exotic, moist flavors of ocean whitefish with shrimp and chicken liver with tuna and salmon with cheese, he was secure. And there was, finally, that which made this new landscape so familiar; it was a sachet of alcohols and aldehydes, of acids and esters, of methane and sulfur. It was the smell of death.

Rag turned and walked down the hall of constant

light, the pastel walls hung with pale, transparent watercolor paintings of stiff flowers and flat fruit, awkwardly rendered by the Buckle Valley Cowbelles, the Buckle River 4-H, and the Buckle High School Art Club. His tail swaggered as he tiptoed along. He pressed his tattered ears forward, the destroyed triangles of them listening for new sounds; his mottled lips were slightly opened to help his nose draw in that smell he knew so well. Walking first under a gurney with a crumpled sheet and then around a wheelchair with a food-stained and stiffened burgundy cardigan dangling over its arm, he stopped at room 113, whose door was ajar. Sticking his head into the darkness, Rag listened to the soft mutterings of Reba Meagher and the tepid breathing of Viola Marsden and twitched his whiskers as he breathed in the scents. It was there, the smell, but not enough to keep him, so he snaked his body around and walked, passing 115, 117, zigging over to 124, zagging back to 127, turning the corner and finally stopping at 141, where he slipped from the hall's blandness into the room that throbbed with night.

The curtains, flesh-colored cloth backed with vinyl to turn away anything natural, had at 8:30—bedtime at the facility—been left open by a sullen male aide. They were open at the request of Teddy Blue, who inhabited 141.

Teddy, whose right side had been paralyzed by the stroke of a summer morning two years before, had in his slurred speech asked that he be slightly propped in bed so that he could see out the bare window, and that the pane be slightly opened, as well. He knew that the aide would do this, not out of any fondness for him but out of a total disregard of the facility's rules. When the young man lifted Teddy by the top of his shoulders, his full-fleshed, brutal young hands crushing the old man's hollowing bones, and then dropped him back against the crooked pillow, Teddy grimaced but did not cry.

Now, at 11:33 and 51, 52, 53, 54 seconds on the fourteenth of June, now at 11:34 and 1, 2, 3—the red numbers blinked away time he no longer felt passing, could no longer feel at all—Teddy waited. He let his eyes travel to a picture on the wall, one of the many hung by his kids, themselves in their sixties now, to make him feel at home. Didn't they understand how much it hurt to feel? There in the frame he posed, cowboy hat jauntily tipped back on his head, a lock of black hair curling on his forehead like a comma, like a pause in the long sentence of his life, and a black-and-white border collie by his booted foot. Was it Mitts or Roxy or Spats or or or or or . . . how many dogs had marked the terms of his life, 11:36 and 15, 16, 17 . . . Mitts and Roxy and Spats and what was that one's name, the one with the one brown and one blue eye . . . Mitts and Roxy and Spats and 52, 53, 54, and there he was with Mitts or Roxy or Spats or that one with the different eyes, what was its name, staring out to the future, out to now, didn't have a clue about strokes, didn't know an old man would be staring back at him. "Damn fool," he slurred at the young man he didn't know anymore, and Rag jumped on the bed. The jump was solid and assured.

"Knew you comin', you sumabitch," Teddy muttered at the cat as it circled. He admired the suppleness of its spine as it turned and turned, the short tail puffed out and twitching, turned and turned, and Teddy looked at the red numbers—11:37 and 30, 31, 32, and the tail twitched and turned, rubbing against his nose, making him want to sneeze, and he felt the able half of his mouth smile because the tickle reminded him of sex, a build-up before an explosion, sex he hadn't had in over a quarter century, watched as the patch tabby turned and turned, then stopped and hunched over its front legs which were pressed into his senseless arm, the paws kneading his pajamas, the talons folding and unfolding into crumpled cotton and then wrinkled flesh, drawing blood and sensation bright as the moon to Teddy. One more time the cat turned and then tucked its legs under itself, curling into a fur ball in the old man's armpit, its head stretched across his breast, the one eye staring at his face, the whiskers trembling as its feral nose sniffed the old man's breath.

"Sumabitch," Teddy tried to whisper, and, had his right arm worked, he would have reached it over to stroke the thick coat of the damned thing. 11:42 and 19, 20, 21. The young man in the cowboy hat looked out at him, a curl of hair upon his forehead, a border collie, was it Mitts or Roxy or Spats or that one with one brown and one blue eye? A moon eye. That was it; the name was Moon. It was full and blue, the moon. Teddy could feel his arrhythmic heart purr; or was it the cat? He looked down at the full, yellow eye and then out the window as the cat tucked into his neck, as if it could keep him warm.

Rag kept Teddy company until he stopped breathing. And then he jumped from the bed and onto the sill of the opened window, where he sat and tentatively stretched his head into the rich night. For a moment his muscular body strained toward it, but then he settled back on his haunches and, turning, hopped down into the room full of moonlight and silence, eventually winnowing out the crack in the door.

On nimble feet he walked straight down the long hallway to the station and the nurse who still dozed over her article. He went to his water bowl and lapped daintily, then, settling into his bed near the file cabinet, under the ascetic lights, he yawned, a sharp canine—the other had just recently festered and been taken out by Doc McTee—flashing. And he slowly closed his eye.

Conjugations of the Verb To Be

29 ACROSS. *EXISTS*.

Is, she scratched with a #2 wooden pencil her husband had probably tried to sharpen with a knife since there were no true sharpeners in the town house they had moved into. Because of the dullness of the tip, her answer was more an indentation than a commitment, and that seemed to Bea Easton indicative of her life. She was fifty-nine years old and barely making a mark on the world.

30 Across. Katie Couric's station.

Katie Couric. Now, Katie was making a mark on the world. No Keatsian lament there, no "my name is writ in water" or, in Bea's case, "my name is writ with a dull pencil." She thought of reaching across the table to grab the mechanical one, the implement with which she had been grading papers, but it would require effort, so Bea pressed hard, and a shadowy *CBS* appeared. "What are you doing?" she asked herself. It was 4:03 in the afternoon; she hadn't looked at an essay since morning, and that one lay to the left of her, where she had discarded it after reading: "To me, the American Dream is a mixture of things put together plus some other extra things added into. It is the right to freedom, the option for choices, the land of opportunity and things like that that lets an individual be individuals. I think that is defiantly what the Declaration of Independence states: that we all have the right to things. If people can have things and do things, than they are really really living the American dream." She had come to this development at the bottom of page one of Staci Cook's essay and, realizing she had four more pages to read, had, as Staci would spell it, *defiantly* given up. Staci was a pimpled, round-faced nineteen-year-old who imagined being a doctor, as she was, she bragged the first day of class, a pre-med student. They all started out as pre-med or engineering students, but by the end of freshman year, they became accounting or education majors.

Bea couldn't imagine Staci, who yawned and texted and turned to check the classroom clock from 12:45 to 2:00 every Tuesday and Thursday, being much of anything, let alone . . . well . . . anything. The thought of her checking a patient ("I know there's a heart in here somewhere"), or a teacher ("Write a paragraph that describes *things*"), or an accountant—her accountant—looking over the mess that was Tim's and her life ("If I were you, I'd just really really shoot myself. Defiantly!") frightened Bea.

But first it angered her. As she felt the rush of adrenaline, the rush that arose from absolute hatred of poor deluded Staci, she also knew that it came from fear. What were she and Tim going to do?

31 Across. Edward of *Twilight*.

The newspaper ripped as Bea pressed down hard to imprint a *v*. "Shit." As she more lightly scratched the remaining *ampire*, she wondered how someone like Stephenie Meyer could be visited by dreams of vampires, dreams she wrote down day in and day out, the series of books and films turning her into a millionaire. Meanwhile, she, Bea, wrote considerate and *really, really* thoughtful stories, which no one but a few obscure literary journals condescended to carry, which was why she had been and would forever be relegated to what she called "the big house on the hill," but what others called Limon Hall on the campus of Rockmount State University.

When strangers at cocktail parties asked her what she did and she answered that she taught composition at the university, Bea could typically watch one of two expressions form on their faces: fear that they would speak ungrammatically, which they undoubtedly would ("Between you and I, I was never very good at English"), or acceptance, because they believed her to be on equal socioeconomic footing with themselves. Bea and Tim somehow managed to be invited to gatherings by people who owned second homes in Big Springs, which had become a lifestyle destination, or by people who knew people who owned second homes and who wanted to have friends from the community who were up to par, so to speak. That Bea published—even in obscure literary journals—helped.

What she never told them was that she was not a professor but an adjunct. *Adjunct*. The social circle whose
perimeter she had for years nervously paced would not
envision her as an adjunct, because she simply would not
allow it. She did not want anyone to know her as "something added to another thing but not essential to it"; or
as "a person associated with lesser status, rank, authority,
etc., in some duty or service"; or as "an assistant; a person working at an institution, at a college or university,
without having full status: *Bea works two days a week as
an adjunct, teaching writing to students like Staci Cook. In
privacy, she calls herself an abject.*"

32 Across. A word in the Cartesian anthem.

The nub of pencil wavered above the two spaces allot-
ted. Bea completed the crossword puzzles that ran in the
Daily Chronicle Monday through Saturday specifically
because they were minimally challenging. She liked to
look at the time suggested for completion, usually between twenty-two and twenty-six minutes, and finish in
ten or twelve. She never attempted the Sunday puzzle
because it was too hard; she wanted just enough of a
challenge to ward off Alzheimer's, assuming a facility
with language could keep that disease at bay. In fact, she
often encouraged her students to challenge themselves
with more complex diction and sentence structures, telling them of the convent of old nuns who were studied by
doctors actually smart enough to have become doctors.
What was discovered was that the nuns who had bigger
vocabularies and who could create sentences other than
simple declarative ones did not develop Alzheimer's; the
rest of the pack did. This semester, she had forestalled

presenting this information in class because she hoped Staci Cook would develop the disease. That the other nineteen students could be, as the military liked to call such people, collateral damage . . . well, so be it. They weren't very interesting, either.

Bea moved to the Down column to help her out with this small Cartesian impasse.

21 Down. Oral e.g.

Sex. Bea thought how lucky she was that her pencil had no lead, as she did not have to erase her answer, which filled only three of the four spaces demanded. And how silly of her. Sex would only be a proper response for *Gender*. Sex was not something people do; it certainly was not what she and Tim did. How *really really defiantly* silly of her! What had she been thinking?

Think . . .

32 Across. A word in the Cartesian anthem.

Am. "I think; therefore, I am," Descartes had proclaimed. Two spaces. *Am*. Which meant 29 Down. Oral e.g. did have an e and an x but no s. Of course. *Exam*. As if exams were what normal human beings would think. What Bea thought was that in—she turned her head to look at the clock, just as Staci Cook incessantly did from 12:45 to 2:00 every Tuesday and Thursday—just thirty-seven minutes, because then it would be 4:47, and she could fix the first of her two martinis. By the time she got the ice out and the gin and the vermouth and the olives and anally measured the ingredients to achieve just the right balance of bitterness and piquancy, it would be 5:00. And she never drank before 5:00. Then she would sit down to watch Katie Couric deliver the news. She didn't really like Katie, who chose to turn the twenty-three minutes stuffed between ads for erectile dysfunction and fibromyalgia and heart attacks and pants wetting into fluff. It was as if there were no war in Afghanistan, as if there were no unemployed or underemployed, as if there were no Tims—sixty-two-years-old and self-employed, which with the recession meant barely employed, and who now sucked air, *really really* sucked the fucking air that stagnated beyond the enclosed HDTV box Katie reported from.

What Bea told everyone was that she didn't like television and that Tim, who was drawn to its flickering like a moth to flame, would never get out the door if they had good reception. But the truth was that cable was too expensive for them right now, so with the new digital broadcasting, the only channel they were capable of getting, because the property manager of the town house they rented said no exterior antennae were allowed, was CBS. And Katie. And fluff. And the martini. "I drink, therefore, I am," she muttered.

And what she also told everyone was that they had grown tired of maintaining their old house, as if after twenty years this phenomenon would occur, just when renovations were finally complete. What they really wanted, Bea continued, was something they didn't have to take care of anymore, like a town house.

Why not buy a condo, everyone asked, and she breezily waved her hand, explaining that they were "keeping options open," that they were thinking of traveling or buying something sleek and sexy, something totally different from their old cottage, as she elected to call it. Tim told everyone that they were "downsizing," gesturing with his hands to create the quotation marks and making it obvious that what he said was a bald-faced lie. Which, of course, it was. The house they had barely managed to sell the year before had little more than 1,500 square feet of tiny, cut-up rooms, and the ceilings were less than eight feet tall. How could they possibly downsize from that?

Of the four Eastons, Bea was the shortest at five-eight. Tim was six-two, their son, Timtoo, six-one, and their daughter, Gussie, six feet, making the rooms seem even more shrunken. This had been all right, though, because the house was in the desirable part of town, city center, near the university, so people like her—professors and whatnot—could walk to work. Just a block away, in a beautiful Tudor-style house that popped up three stories, each one having ten-foot ceilings, lived a professor with whom Bea sometimes walked to campus. This man was in Business, which meant his salary was really greater than that of tenured English professors and *really really* greater than her abject one. It just is so unfair! Bea often thought as she walked with him, bending her ear to his upturned face with the guppy mouth. She walked along tilted toward him not because she was deferential but because she was so much taller. And more than the disparity of salary, what upset Bea was the disparity of heights. The business prof was probably three inches shorter than Bea, his wife shorter than he, and the children of even smaller stature. While these midgets wandered the sundry floors of their expansive house, the Eastons—Andre the Giant and his clan—were stuffed into theirs. Everyone always said that the house was so cozy, but Bea sensed they meant something quite different.

33 Across. A city in Nebraska.

"This is just too easy," Bea said, for she had been conceived in that state. But it was also odd, as usually a city in Oklahoma—Ada, to be exact—was asked for. Counting five spaces, she was a bit disappointed, as Beatrice was not what they were after; indeed, *Beatrice* was never sought out. *Omaha*. She moved to 28 Down to check her answer. The sound of laughter. *Haha*.

There was nothing funny to Bea about her name. She hated it. "Where it all began," she remembered her father telling her, as if she were an *it*, "was in Beatrice. Your mom and I were moving to Chicago from Denver—our first big break—and we spent the night in Beatrice. Oh, what a night," he winked. "You'll always remind me of that night!" She was twelve when her dad told her of her origin, and she was appalled on three counts: the first was the universal revulsion all children have at the visual of their parents doing it; the second was that something as private as her very beginning should be made public, even though the public consisted only of her and her mother, who was looking quite chagrined; the third was that with just a little imagination they could have called her *BE*atrice, emphasis on the first syllable, so people would believe her to be named after Dante's beautiful guide in the *Divine Comedy*; instead, they named her Be*AT*rice, just as the denizens of the city they would never ever go through again pronounced it.

Just the week before Bea had been at a party at the Madison Club, a gated community for the *über*rich. Because she was a friend of a friend of one of the Realtors, she'd been invited to this function at one of the many cabins, which were in actuality ten-thousand-square-foot log houses that the owners liked to call cabins. They talked like they were homesteaders who had been out a-hewin' and a-notchin' logs and then come in and cleaned and blinged up. At this party, she was introduced to a lithe woman with a subtle sienna complexion, Caribbean blue eyes, and sleek black hair. The sleek woman explained how she and her husband were out at their cabin for a few weeks before they returned to Connecticut. Greenwich, to be exact. Her name was Cuba, she said, named for the island of her conception during the missile crisis in 1962. Her mother was Cuban, her father CIA. Bea imagined the water, the sky, the palms, the sand, the music, the tension of that night, even as she remembered how she had looked up Beatrice, Nebraska, at the library after her father had dealt her her humility. It was known for its services to the mentally handicapped and for its feedlot.

A man, another homesteader at the Club who looked to be about Bea's age, was listening to tropical Cuba's story. When she finished, he volunteered that his wife, a stunning woman younger than he by at least a quarter century and standing next to him, was named Margaux, after the bottle of wine her parents had been drinking in France when she was conceived. Putting his arm around her, he buried his head in her simply coiffed blond hair, breathing her in. "She has a full-flavored bouquet and a magnificent elegance," he announced, and everyone laughed. Then looking to Bea, he pronounced, "*BE*a-trice" (that is how she'd introduced herself). "Your parents must have been reading *Paradise Lost* when you were

conceived." Knowing that Tim was across the room talking animatedly with others, she concurred. Later in the
evening, she saw him speaking with Mr. Margaux, and
she internally grimaced as she watched him raise both
hands to gesture quotation marks. "'*BE*atrice' is not the
correct pronunciation," she'd imagined him saying. "It's
Be*AT*rice." And if not that, "We decided to 'downsize.'"

49 Across. "To be ——— to be."

Or not. This was too easy. Bea swung to look at the
clock. It would not take her more than five minutes to
complete this puzzle, leaving at least twenty until it was
4:47. And that meant she would have to read Staci Cook's
essay. Or not. She could skim the pages, making at least
one mechanical correction per page. Then she could
bend the stapled left hand corner so it appeared that she
had folded the essay back as she read, giving each "development" of Staci's serious consideration. After all, at
the end of the semester Staci would evaluate her: Had
Staci been entertained? Had her teacher shown mastery
of the subject? Had Staci been fairly graded? Was there
anything Staci would like the teacher to do differently?
Would Staci care for anything, anything at all?

Staci, like most of the students Bea encountered,
would graduate with $30,000 (the cost of one year at
Rockmount State) of debt; this would be in addition
to the $90,000 paid in the process of getting educated,
which for Staci meant maybe learning that *defiantly* was
not *definitely*, perhaps coming to understand that *really*
really really didn't help qualify verbs or adjectives, even
when used twice; and possibly considering synonyms for
things. Her grade, according to one of Bea's supervisors,

was to be determined by her "arc of learning." Bea understood this to mean that Staci had better not flunk the class; the administration, ubiquitous and growing by 10 percent over the course of five years, did not like students (could it be a verb?) attriting. Failing. Dropping out. Transferring. "Things like that," as Staci might say, "defiantly makes them really really unhappy."

Bea knew her time was running out—not in completing the puzzle but in teaching. She just didn't have the energy to keep the Stacis of the world entertained anymore, and the age gap was growing too great. At fifty-nine, she was almost old enough to be a grandmother to many of them, but she didn't have the bust or the nurturing personality for that. Nor did the young of America equate age with sagacity. She would have to quit. But how? What could she do? She would have to be something else, as Tim brought in virtually nothing. Become a greeter at Walmart or McDonald's? There was so little one could do in Big Springs, there was so little to be.

55 Across. Latin 101 word.

Amo. "I love . . . ," Bea said quietly, but she couldn't think of a direct object with which to complete the sentence. Though Tim's name had come to mind, she maliciously deleted it as that part of speech. She supposed she could just love in general, but she knew that she didn't. She would never be Mother Teresa. But *Amo* was one letter too short, so she didn't have to worry about it. *Amas?* "You love." Was the "you" specific or general? Who loved? And could she be the direct object? She had, after all, become hateful. Really really defiantly hateful.

On purpose. That could be it. *Amas*, she pressed in.

46 Down. Biography.

"Damn," Bea whispered. That meant *Amas* was wrong. But no worry. Since there was not a mote of lead left, no mistake had been made. There was nothing to erase. Had she not lived, Bea thought, there would be no mistakes, nothing to erase. As it were, however . . . 46 Down. *Life*. And that meant that 55 Across was . . .

45 Down. Bigwigs on campus.

Profs. Easy enough. And that meant that 55 Across was . . . a Latin 101 word. "Hmmm."

The leadless pencil slightly trembled to the beat of Bea's heart, the rush of her blood, as she held it in her hand. Then, *Esse*—being—she entered as best she could.

"*J'ai fini!*" Bea turned to look at the clock, which registered 4:23. Because it had taken her only fourteen minutes, she was pleased. But then, remembering Staci Cook's essay, she sighed. Certainly she could finish that within twenty-four minutes, when it would be 4:47, which meant she could begin to fix the first of her two martinis before she sat down to watch Katie Couric's news.

Romance Writer

WHAT, I WONDER, WAS ELLIS THINKING ABOUT THIS MORN-
ing, with the June sun reflecting off the neighbor's siding into our bedroom, gilding everything in an exagger-
ated light. He is, after all, sanguine in both complexion
and attitude, and had I been turned to him with my eyes
open, I imagine I would have seen him ruddy in the rich-
ness of the morning, and we might have talked and I
might have known rather than imagined. But, over the
course of this year, I've grown out of the habit of turning
toward him for much of anything—including his version of the truth. And, I suppose, he has grown out of the
habit of expecting me to. A secret can do that to a couple.

Ellis moves through the world with liquid ease; he always has, and this is one of the reasons I married him.
Even after twenty-six years, what I find attractive in him
hasn't gone away; somewhere along the line, I just began

to qualify it. Let me use an analogy. Ellis's ease is like that of a leaf—a green one, never anything but an optimistic green—on water; he floats on this world's currents, letting them take him and enjoying the ride; unlike the rest of us, he never seems to get eddied. I always knew this about him, but his lightness—his thinness of personality—his desire only to skate on surfaces, has now taken prominence in my understanding of him.

And who knows; maybe I'm jealous, as I have always been the heavy in this marriage: the rock. When I was growing up on the ranch, there was a pool in the river, and Tillie and I would play there quite often. While the water seemed still because of its depth, there was actually a strong current, and to get across it, I would grab a rock from the bank and, holding on to it, hurl it forward. Its heft would pull me to the bottom of the pool, of course, and then, as quickly as I could, I would surface with the rock over my head and throw it again. Sometimes, while Tillie skipped along the bank to the shallows, I would spend a half an hour crossing thirty feet of water, getting dragged down by the weight I had voluntarily taken on, skinning my knuckles as my rock crashed with an echoed hollowness into those resting in the riverbed.

One of Ellis's and my basic differences, then—at least by my lights—is that my husband can be described in two lines; I just gave myself ten, and when I surface, I'm still throwing myself into depths of my own making. I, of course, composed the metaphors, so there's no reason I should be trusted. I am, by all accounts, an unreliable narrator.

An unreliable narrator is a luxury I can't afford in

my line of work. I'm a romance writer; I do historical romances. My fans know me as Rose Poignard, a very reliable narrator, not as Helena Como, a forty-eight-year-old wife whose marriage is failing.

My readers, God love them, do not like failed marriages or first-person limited points of view. They like third-person omniscient, allowing them to see not only into the heroine's head but into the hero's. They like to see how each misunderstands the other, which creates a delay in the couple's coming together in love but at the same time promises the audience that they all—readers and characters—will get to that point, to that romance ... But in their own real lives, which is what my audience wants to escape when they pick up one of my books, and in my own real life, how can we be anything but limited and unreliable?

So. Unreliably, this is what I imagine Ellis was thinking about this morning: how yesterday he birdied the thirteenth hole at the club; if after I left this morning for my writing studio, he would arrange to meet Alice; how long till her boys come home from their Mount Hood camp and, laggards that they are, plop themselves in front of their gaming devices; how intellectually stunted they are compared to our own Ty and Bessie and Ria and what that suggests about Alice that he doesn't already know; how fast she can come in bed, even though she's just two years younger than I am; how he wishes I were still so eager; whether he will use Warren on the North Side redevelopment project, or David, even though his plans aren't as good as Warren's; why reputation, which David has and Warren doesn't, is important; how with David at dinner last night, Ellis could tell asparagus was in season by the smell in the men's room; when Ria, just a tiny little thing but so bright and quick, had first told us pee smelled different after eating asparagus.

When I glance over what I've written, I can see that I'm not being unkind to him. I have imagined that, even though they are superficial, his thoughts are far ranging and that he loves our children very much.

So. He had lain there, desultory in the yolked light as I pretended to sleep on in a darkness that more and more seems of my own making. More practical than he likes to admit, Ellis checked off those thoughts—*thinks* Bessie used to call them—that were done deals. There was no denying that asparagus chemically reacts with urine to create a unique smell, or that Alice's boys are idiots and he will never have them work under, let alone with, him. This is reserved for Ty, who is living in misery in some Los Angeles flat trying to make it as a novelist because his mother, who at his age couldn't afford the luxury of writing stories of how the human heart really works, subsidizes him.

Finally, what Ellis was left with was a small flock of unresolved ideas, and he lined them up like birds on a wire in order of importance, eager to start knocking them off now that he had them in his sights.

Alice first. As he has done through the years when it comes to sex, he decided to let me make the decision for him. Coming up on his elbow, Ellis studied me to see how deeply asleep I was and to what degree that might affect my mood, which had been bad the night before. I could feel him looking down on me.

What I suspect he noticed first were the shadows—

cubist in design, created by the cross of windowpanes—upon my face. Then he examined the downturn of lips and the small scratches of lines that ran into them; a track running from each side of my nose to the corners of my mouth, laid with rails of sadness and happiness that even in relaxation never go away now; the crow's-feet perched on the edge of my eyes. My falsely colored and highlighted hair fell back from my right ear, where he could see the small white stitch marks of the cosmetic surgeon.

Brave? he probably wondered. Is Helena brave? Was it courage or cowardice to try to fight time? The operative word was *try*, for after the facelift, the shape of my eyes have become just a wee bit Oriental, and there is that constant and certain tension to my mouth that was not there before. Though most of my acquaintances would not be aware of such subtle differences, Ellis, who once loved me intimately and thoroughly, is, and it has unnerved him.

Even though he's unnerved, I think my husband would say that never has he been out of love with me. And never has he been in love with anyone like Alice, any more than Columbus loved Hispániola but not Spain. But for some reason, now in our marriage, he has a need to explore her, to map the topography of *her* body. As far as I know, in our twenty-six years together, he has not been a womanizer, an exploiter; he is not like the male heroes of my novels, the Gavins and Devons and Beauregards and Geoffreys who desire conquest and who, in those initial moments after navigating the treacherous waters that surround the many unimportant female characters with whom they must sleep, find ways to draw near without wrecking. But like my heroes, Ellis would say that only when he is once again moored near his only love—me—does he feel he is home, complete, and safe.

Thus, the slight change in my face from the cosmetic surgery makes him feel as if he's reached landfall only to find the shoreline changed, which has cast in doubt his ability to navigate that which for "one score and six," as my latest hero, cavalry officer Anton Chrétien, would say, has been the one constant in his life.

Until a year ago, after my plastic surgery, when Ellis made love to me, he always kept his eyes open, reveling in my whole familiar geography, the rich culture I have let him live in. Now, however, he keeps them closed, trusting his instincts, as well as his familiarity of my inlets and tides, to lead him where he needs to be.

I could feel Ellis tip back onto his pillow, and I imagined him staring at the ceiling, squeezing his lips together in concentration and then shrugging his eyebrows as he would his shoulders, which is part of his facial choreography when he's thinking. Then he rolled onto his side again and pursed his lips at the nape of my neck as he encircled me in an arm. From years of touching me, the arm knew at exactly what angle it must hinge itself so that his hand could come to rest on my breast, which, pressed by the mattress, felt bigger than it is. He squeezed it, grateful that I've had the good sense not to alter that, for while in romances the women are always pulchritudinous, they also never age past twenty-five, let alone past forty, when pulchritude morphs to two dangling despairs.

Of course such pressure would wake me. But unknown these days—to me and to him—has been whether I will be pleased or annoyed, and thus his decision on whether to meet Alice after I leave for my studio.

Keeping his lips pursed and pressed to me, taking in the scent of hibiscus in my hair, Ellis waited. He moved his thumb slightly so that it rested against my sternum, allowing him to feel any change of rhythm in my breathing.

There it was, just the merest hitch. He knew I was awake, even as I feigned sleep.

Was he grateful to maintain the pretense? All I know is that he gently lifted his arm from me and slid from under the summer comforter, padding across the room to the master bathroom. Alice it is; I'm sure it is. Right now; right this minute.

THIS IS HOW I CAME to possess the secret of Ellis's affair with Alice.

It was last year, morning, on the first day of autumn, September 21, and I was going to the post office to get my manuscript off to Dottie Llewellyn at Journoman and money off to our Bessie. The night before, she had called needing to pay her college tuition, and Ellis and I—pleased that she was returning to college, pleased that she was doing something other than waiting on that self-absorbed man she'd married, pleased that she was again including us in her life—were eagerly generous.

As I drove east into the sun, bobbing my head to squint through the dusty windshield, I stopped for an old woman in a maroon Buick trying to parallel park in front of the post office. And then, at that hour of day that is so lovely on the fall equinox, in the midst of a happy task, the secret unfolded before me.

At first I wasn't sure, given the dust and light on the windshield, but the woman just coming out of the post office was Alice. I recognized her because of her hair, which is much too young for her. It is naturally curly, and through the years, she has permanently enhanced the curls and added highlights. They hang shaggily— quite wildly, really—down around her shoulders. From the back, it makes her look quite young, but that may be because she's worn her hair that way since I first met her, and so it seems a hairdo for a thirty-something woman. And when she turns around and you see the wrinkles and sunspots one gets from leading what our culture considers a leisurely life, it just doesn't work. The hair-do, I mean. I like the lifestyle as much as anyone.

I smiled. As much as I love—well, *loved*—her, the hairdo has always made me feel superior to her, despite the fact that I'm a romance writer and she's a neuropsy-chologist. As sophisticated as she appears—she's English and had lived all over the world until she settled here with Richard, her husband, about twelve years ago—the hair established that she couldn't quite present herself honestly. Everything else about her is perfect, of course. She dresses as simply as I do, if a little more provoca-tively because she has more bosom. A typical outfit for her is a pair of khaki pants and a knit top with a V-neck, and—of course—her cleavage, into which drops a string of pearls or a gold necklace. There is always something dropping in there, and until last fall, I never dreamed it would be my husband. Anyway, except for what dangles around her neck, the constancy and uniformity of her clothing makes it seem as if she doesn't care, as if she's above all this fray, as if she has too many things on her mind to bother with the frivolity of style.

So that day, I was thinking of her as being less than perfect. But since I've come to possess the secret, I've noticed other telltale signs of imperfection. For example, the four of us, Richard and Alice and Ellis and I, met just a week ago for cocktails at their house before we went to a film society offering. Because I now have trouble looking her in the eye, I was staring at her feet, and I noticed that she has a bunion on her left one. And the skin on both her heels is as thick and cracked as an elephant's.

I am sounding unreliable again, and petty. After all, though I've tried, I'm less than perfect. And I'd be the first to say so. I mean, really. Look at Bessie. She's been out of touch with us for quite a while; obviously, I've not been a perfect mother. If I had been, she'd love us for more than the money she now needs.

And our Ty is a nice boy, though he thinks he's a man. By law, he is; he's twenty-one. Before he was legally a man, however—when he was barely nineteen—he met a woman fourteen years older than he. Yes, Patricia is old enough to be his mother, at least by some morally impoverished standards. Or at least his babysitter.

Ty was the cutest little boy, and, like many little boys, he loved dinosaurs. When he was five, he could name and spell them all, and I shake my head and wonder what I did to lose him, and when it happened. In the present tense of memory, I see him as he was fifteen years ago: his tongue sticking out of his little pursed lips as his sticky fingers grasp his thick pencil and he practices writing in his Big Chief notebook R-E-X. R-E-X. And fifteen years ago, two thousand miles away, Patricia's in college, maintaining only a 2.0 GPA—she's laughingly told me that's all she ever maintained—as she focuses on S-E-X. S-E-X. Ellis tells me not to worry, that it wasn't my mothering or lack of it, that it was God or Fate or Karma or Destiny that took its miserable, long-nailed finger and Etch A Sketched the wobbly lines of their lives across the grainy screen of America and had them cross.

Accidents like this don't happen in my romances. In fact, I would lose my fans if my heroines were cougars. In my books, which the trade calls "sweet savage romances" or "bodice rippers" or "erotic historicals" (Ellis calls them "erratic hystericals"), the heroine is usually about eighteen when she encounters the hero, who is anywhere from eight to twelve years older than she; he is schooled in sex but not in love, while she daydreams about love but not sex. They, of course, throughout the course of the novel, must each be awakened to the other's kind of love: he to emotion and she to physicality. Then, as fully realized human beings, they enter a fully realized relationship, which is what all my readers hunger for.

Just two weeks ago, I received this:

Dear Miss Poignard,

I am twenty-three. I am a wife and I am a mother of two, and sometimes, not because I'm a wife and a mother

but because I'm just a regular person, I get depressed, may-
be from hearing something bad on the radio or television or
maybe because someone has been mean to me, or etcetera.
That is when I can pick up one of your books, like Flowers
on the Waves, and see all the goodness staring out at me.
Dorothea, who is just like me, helps me remember that it's a
nice world, and people are good and one can face any hard-
ship and overcome it and we are all lucky to be alive. What
a wonderful feeling! If it wasn't for you, I'd never know this
uplift. Your books stand for decency and belief, and that's
real rare these days.

Sincerely,

Vicki Flemming

Vicki, just three years older than our Ria and already
a mother of two, would not buy my books if their stories
resembled Ty's life (or Ria's, who at the moment lives in
an abbey in Nebraska and meditates, seeking not physical or emotional love but agape). Ty's story would not
help her remember that it's a nice world and people are
good and one can face any hardship and we are all lucky
to be alive.

Interestingly, most of the people with whom I social-
ize believe I write romances because that is how my life
is: my art (such as it is) imitates life. With them, there is
no comfortable way to present the small, tawdry secret I
have come to possess.

Yes. The secret. So I was peering through the dust
drops of the windshield, and Alice came out of the post

office. I watched her open the door of a car I couldn't see, as it was blocked by the old lady trying to parallel park her purple Buick.

Waiting patiently and benignly, aware that my good humor grew out of the fact that Bessie once again needed us, hopeful that if she was changing Ty could, too, I thought of the fall equinox and what it means. Balance. The world, just two times a year, in the spring and in the autumn, is perfectly balanced—not too much light, not too much dark. And it was just for a day: no more than a day. Or, in my case, a mere few hours, for balance was about to end.

The sun dappled my face, warming me just a little, as the car Alice hopped into, its blinker signaling to the world its intent, became visible.

It was Ellis's. My husband's car. And my husband was driving it. My husband. As he unself-consciously pulled away, I saw Alice's maddening curls move toward him and cover half his head. Though I could not see clearly, what I have imagined happening, again and again, is her sun-spotted face pulling next to his, her lips pursing, maybe the tongue sticking out as she licks his sandpapery cheek.

It's late June now; in fact, tomorrow is summer solstice. And I surmise Ellis and Alice are still together when they can be, though I don't know for sure. This is because I have kept the secret to myself.

I have, over the past few months, on days when I can barely stand it, wondered why I have done this.

In a word, power. When one possesses a secret, one

possesses power. I remember this from my own childhood. When I had a secret and wanted to tell someone
or everyone, I nevertheless clenched it tight in my teeth
and balled it up in my tongue, and it was as big and solid
and juicy as a wad of bubble gum. I chewed on the idea
that only I knew.

My power, however, is accompanied by a kind of
Promethean pain. I am chained to this situation that
eats away at my liver. I say liver instead of heart, the ac-
knowledged organ of love, because that's what happened
to Prometheus. Every day an eagle would come and feed
on his liver, and every night it would grow back. In the
morning, then, he would wake up, still chained to a rock
and to his knowledge, and imagine the gnawing pain he
would again face. That's how I wake up now—whole
but not for long. In fact, I wake up, and just like that, I
feel myself diminishing. And, besides that, I'm drinking
quite heavily, so this whole affair is probably damaging
my liver in a physical as well as metaphysical way.

But back to the secret. Just as Prometheus gained
knowledge, that's what I've gained. And, as I've said,
knowledge, however painful, is power. I mean, it has to
be; why else would anyone want it?

I'm sure it is, because I can see things no one else can.
For example, during cocktails last week, beyond notic-
ing Alice's white elephant feet and her bunion, I noticed
the way Ellis looked at her as we all talked in their kitch-
en. It's the way he used to look at me. It's a look I had
forgotten.

It's all in the eyes, which, without speech, confess the
secrets of the heart. This is how the confession looks:

even though the eyes are wide open, there's a quality of them being tightly focused, of trying hard to see, to understand. This was the hard part, this knowledge that Ellis was trying hard to see Alice instead of me, which meant that I was boring to him, and who knows, maybe I am. After all, I spend my time writing about simple love between simple people. Or maybe he no longer cares if he understands me. Anyway, his iris was lit up like a wick in a candle, and I stood there in the shadow, just beyond the arc of light Ellis was throwing.

In the darkness, then, privy to the light he cast like a lighthouse out to Alice, I felt this hollowness, not the kind my heroines get when they want the heroes to sexually fulfill them but are too simple and innocent to know what the feeling is, but the kind you get when you're . . . well . . . getting your liver pecked out.

I looked at Richard to see if he saw what I did, that his male pal Ellis was without an iota of conscience cuckolding him (cuckold is a word I use with abandon in my novels; my readers, once they look it up, love it), but Richard just went glibly on, talking about the film we would be seeing.

When we got to the theater, poor Richard said to Ellis, "Why don't you sit next to Alice so you two get a chance to talk."

It made me wonder what they talk about when they're together. What do people who have been friends for twelve years and then become lovers talk about? Is there more to say than if you've been lovers and then become whatever Ellis and I are? Do they talk about us, about Richard and me and how boring and simple we are?

As I sat in the darkened theater, I looked at Richard, engrossed and slipping a kernel of popcorn into his mouth and chewing it quietly, his eyes focused on all the wrong things, missing out on the skirmishes going on along his home front, and he did seem ... well ... simple. Boring.

Then I turned to my right and looked at Ellis. I put my knee against his and wrapped my hand around his thigh. What had once been so natural, so familiar, was now so self-conscious.

Like Richard, Ellis never turned away from the screen, though he did grab my hand and squeeze it. It was as warm as ever, as comforting as it once had been.

How could he, I thought, how could he warmly hold my hand and do what he was doing? To her, no less? To my friend? I leaned forward and looked past Ellis to Alice, who sat with her hands wrapped around a giant box of jujubes squeezed between her knees. I don't know why, but I couldn't help but imagine her in a bed—what bed, though, where did they go?—with my husband, squeezing him between her hands and knees. My husband, who had become her sweet, various, colorful candy.

Then Ellis patted my hand as he returned it to my lap. Dismissed. I had been dismissed.

When we got home and were hanging our coats in the foyer closet, Ellis asked if I'd like a cup of tea. "No," I said sharply. "Brandy."

"Well, you'll have to get that yourself. I'm going to bed." That is his way of telling me he has noticed how much I drink. He didn't stop me, though. Perhaps he hopes the alcohol will peck out my liver so that as a widower, he can more easily see Alice. Or perhaps Alice is merely his gateway girl, as marijuana is the gateway drug. And having breathed her in, he is eager to try all kinds of women who will more immediately rush his blood.

Unlike in my romances, I do not control this narrative. I only control the secret.

I will say nothing of their choices and tell them nothing of mine. For as I sit in my studio supposedly working on the chapter in which Anton Chrétien and Savannah Lafleur consummate their love but instead imagining Ellis sleeping in our room with Alice, I remind myself that it is still our room, perhaps always our room, as long as both he and I do not spill our beans. A secret, after all, if it is kept, can become a shared relation between people.

Some might say this choice of mine is made of powerlessness rather than power. But isn't it strong to create our lives out of what we hope for, keeping secret our own insufficiencies and sadnesses? Or is it braver when we take our secrets into the world and hand them over to strangers, with the full understanding that the lives from which they spring are too late to reclaim?

Isn't that what serious writers do?

Twin Bridges, Montana

Most children in the state orphanage . . . were never adopted.
—Montana Historical Society

She had fallen on the pond's ice, and that is where she first became aware of his presence, the presence of the boy beneath it. Most of the pond had a frosted and dimpled-glass quality to it, and it was the dimples that had made her trip and fall, those and the oversized hockey skates with the rusty blades and cracked brown leather that the wards could use. She, however, was the only child who did so, for of them all she was the only one who preferred the cold of a day and the solitude of the pond to the loneliness of the orphanage.

Lying flat on the ice, then, her cheek pressed to it, feeling the solid turn to liquid beneath her skin, liking the power that her body, at least, could wield, she stared at eye level across the cold plane. Near the middle of the pond, where she didn't skate because the ice took on the transparency of a window, which she imagined her weight shattering and her body dropping through and into a very cold blackness, she saw an aura of red. It was a surprising tone—gay and summery—in the monochrome of this Sunday in deep winter. Pushing up onto hands and knees, she tentatively crawled toward the hue that emanated from beneath the ice.

When she came over the window, staring out at her from inside the pond was the boy. Though her limbs warmed and her heart beat fast with startle, the girl did not flee. She had, after all, seen much death before; it was what had brought her to the orphanage. On her hands and knees, then, she stared at him in his room. Though the ice blurred him, she could tell that his hair was blond and that his eyes, which were wide open as if he looked on the scene above him with both shock and wonderment, were blue. The red came from his coat (wool, she supposed, and she was envious) that in the bite of some recent day had kept him cozy.

She studied the boy till the air gelled first in cold and then in moonlight, and she recalled that the mistress of the orphanage would paddle her for not following the laws of time and the rules of institution.

When she entered the kitchen and stared into the stern eyes of the mistress, the girl, of course, had a perfect excuse as to why she was tardy. But, instead of reporting what was suspended in the ice, she did as she was told and went to get the paddle. That night, with an empty stomach and a bruised bottom, she looked out the window of the darkened dormitory, across the grounds and past the fence, into the fields and to the craggy black of the cottonwoods and willows, beyond which the pond, and the boy in it, lay. Later, after she had climbed beneath the thin blanket on her cot and wrapped herself into a ball to keep her teeth from chattering, she whispered her secret to the girl who slept beside her. This girl was in the orphanage because her father had run off and her mother could not afford to keep her. The following day, a Monday, after doing their lessons and performing their chores and promising to be timely, the girls took two pairs of skates to go to the pond. The mistress was pleased that the one who often wandered alone had finally made a friend.

When the girls got there, they of course did not skate but walked right to the window in the pond to gaze upon the frozen boy. Though they imagined him to be very handsome, the wavy ice made it difficult to tell, and they considered chipping him out with the blades of their skates to see if their longings were correct. Worried, however, that they might not be, the girls left the skates in the snow on the shore of the pond, unused.

On Thursday, the two girls and a boy, one who had been given up by his father because his stepmother found him unruly, asked permission to go skating. The mistress, worried about two adolescent girls and an unruly boy sequestered in the woods, told them it was ill advised. Quickly they altered their request, explaining how they wanted to take some of the smaller children for an outing, how good it would be for them to get off the grounds. Many of them, they argued, cried themselves to sleep at night, missing mothers and fathers who for one reason or another did not miss them. But we haven't enough skates, the mistress told them. We will take the tin trays from the kitchen and the old chairs from the shed and push them on the ice, showing them a good time, the three pleaded. Smiling, pleased at the turn of events, the mistress watched out the window as the group grew smaller and then disappeared into the distant wood.

When the orphans arrived, the three oldest put the chairs in the middle of the pond and sat down, pulling the smallest ones onto their laps. The others circled the trays around the clear ice and sat. Except for a magpie in a willow, no one cried; they all just stared through the window at the boy who stared back. Finally, one of the little children asked how old he was. Twelve, the girl who first saw him answered, and no one argued because he was her find, so she had dibs on him. And, besides, it was a good age, one they could all identify with, for it made him neither grown-up nor child.

What is his name, another wanted to know, and the unruly boy, who was moved because the frozen one seemed so close in size to him and the age imagined was just a year older than his own, said that they would need to give that some thought.

That evening at supper, the children who had visited the pond were quiet, and their cheeks were rosy. The mistress was pleased. And by Friday afternoon, after lessons were done and chores completed with nary a complaint or a delay, every child in the orphanage, even the one with the withered leg and the other with no sight, asked to go skating. The bigger children said they would carry the weak and the small and would take good care of them all. Delighted at the prospect of the orphanage emptied of all its sadnesses for once, the mistress assented.

When all the orphans were gathered around the window, sitting on chairs and trays and each other, the blind child asked what the boy beneath the ice looked like. He is very handsome, the first girl told him. He has blue eyes that stare straight out at the world without flinching, a boy told him. His hair is blond and his skin is very pale and unflawed, a girl with a large strawberry birthmark on her face added. He is tall and slender and well balanced in limb, the child with the withered leg explained. And he has a smile on his face, the blind boy offered. Yes, everyone nodded. Yes, he does.

But what is his name, the child who had wondered the same on the day before asked again. The unruly boy who had answered that some thought was needed was now ready for this. The night before, he had snuck *Good Names to Make Boys and Girls Good* out of the orphanage library and studied it by candle under his bed. Joey. His first name is Joey. Babby is his last. Joey Babby. Breathless, as if he were a father naming his own baby, he waited for complaint. None came. Does he have a middle initial? No. His parents don't believe in them. Why not? Who are they? The questions came quickly from the younger children. They are Mr. and Mrs. Babby, and they wanted his name to be as perfect as he is.

But why is he here? a small child wanted to know. He likes to hunt, a boy, who on the day he was delivered to the orphanage had passed a father shooting clay pigeons with his son, answered. And he wears the red jacket of a hunter. His gun, which is resting in an ornately carved wooden case against the wall down there (and he pointed through the ice window) is a shotgun, 12-gauge, over-and-under barrels, and the metal on the stock is silver.... And etched with figures of his favorite dogs, a girl who missed the pets she used to have added. In fact, his best dog, a white one with brown and black spots, is sleeping near the woodstove, waiting to be whistled.

Where does he live? Here for now. But mostly Joey lives in a home in a big town, a three-story house with twelve-foot-tall ceilings and flowered wallpaper and a fireplace in every room and two front doors that open onto the wraparound verandah where wicker chairs sit. Any evening of a summer you can find him out there with his parents and his brother and sister . . . his best spotted dog at this feet, don't forget his dog, the girl who missed her pets piped in . . . yes, with his dog at his feet and a cat, a great big patch tabby with thick fur, stretched out long on the porch banister, its tail hanging down and twitching the petals of the bachelor buttons and daisies and marigolds and zinnias, as the family sips lemonade and eats chocolate-chip cookies.

But why does Joey want to be here? another little child asked. Doesn't he want to be home in his big bedroom? The one on the third floor, another child added, with the windows that face to the east so he gets the morning light that shines in on his four-poster bed with the comforter two feet deep in goose down. Yes, why doesn't he want to be there instead of here? the one who first asked the question asked again.

Well . . . the big children stalled, they were having trouble with this one . . . because . . .

The little ones waited.

Finally the girl who first found the boy answered. Joey was loved very much. Almost too much. So beloved was he that he felt a terrible responsibility, and it was more than he could bear. And so he chose to be an orphan.

What a strange boy Joey is, another girl commented.

Yes, yes, he is, they all agreed.

Meanwhile, the winter light slipped toward the trees. Quickly, so the mistress would not come looking for them and discover their secret or stop them from coming again because they were late in returning to their broth and bread, the orphans scooped up chairs and trays and the littlest ones and hurried from the pond. Goodbye, Joey, the small ones being toted cried, waving over the shoulders of those who carried them. Goodbye. See you tomorrow! From the woods and through the field and to the outline of their austere home they scurried.

By Sunday, a week after Joey had first been found, the weather began to warm. As the orphans sat through the morning sermon delivered by the visiting preacher, they were restless, for in every sunshined window drops of water teared and then fell from the dangling icicles. When the holy man finally left and the midday dinner was eaten and cleaned up after, they asked the mistress if once again they could all go to the pond. The ice is too soft from the melt, the mistress told them. You might break through and drown.

She was bemused by the smiles her threat brought to their faces. The big children promised to stay off the ice and mind the little ones, and they told her how much better they all felt because of their daily outings. And coming to enjoy the quietude their absence provided, the mistress quickly relented.

At the pond, the children of course ignored the mistress's admonitions. Holding hands, they made a human chain, tentatively working their way out to the window where Joey waited for them, all the while jumping on the sweating ice to test its strength. When the girl who had first discovered him arrived at the window, she let out a dismayed Oh. What? they all cried, and forgetting that they were testing the pond's surface, they dropped each other's hands and ran to see what was the matter. Gathered around, they all repeated Oh, for the pane had lost some of its transparency. Not only was Joey harder to see, but he seemed farther away. Just then, the ice issued a resonant moan, and, frightened, the orphans ran, slipping and sliding and falling, for solid ground. From there they stood through the afternoon, feeling the sun on their heads and shoulders and hating it. That night, none of them could sleep because of the melting ice in the eaves, which tick-tocked drops of water as inexorably as the grandfather clock in the mistress's rooms tick-tocked seconds.

On Monday afternoon, when they all had permission to again go to the pond, the unruly boy, the bravest of them all, ventured onto the slush. On tiptoes he walked, and grasped in his right hand was the threadbare sleeve of a coat, whose other sleeve was tied to a jacket which was belted to a sleeve and so on so that he had a chain of sorts by which those on shore could pull him should he break through the sinking roof of Joey's house. Quietly the children stood, their arms tense with anticipation of rescuing the unruly boy and in dread of losing the frozen one.

Unfortunately, all the coats tied together did not reach the center of the pond. So, cautiously, a child untied one sleeve from another, placing herself as one of the links in the chain. Another child followed, and another, coats and children alternating, as the unruly boy came closer and closer to the window. As it had the day before, the ice moaned, but this time it sank a little, too, with their weight. They ignored it, though, while the soles of their shoes grew wet, and then the leather of them soggy, and their socks soppy. Finally, the unruly boy, leaning forward, could see.

There is just water, he reported. The window has fallen out. And Joey is gone.

The children were silent, until one of the littlest ones said, I want to see. Carefully, they let him take the place at the end of the chain. Standing there, looking into the cold, greasy water, he reached into his pocket and took out his only marble, a mottled blue one as rich as the world to him, and dropped it into the nothingness. Soon all of them were asking to see, and each dropped a possession into the hole—a scarlet ribbon that held back hair, a jackknife used for mumbledypeg, a belt, a pair of socks, a shoelace, another shoelace, a sweater, a coat, shoes. Whatever each child could afford or not was offered.

When they had all returned to shore, they stood staring out where Joey had been. Why did he go? the little ones wailed.

The girl who had first found him tried to find an explanation. Because we loved him. But now, rather than his parents, it is we who loved him too much.

The children were astounded—not only by the thought that there was someone they loved, but that they could love.

That evening, they were late in returning to the orphanage. They arrived happy if disheveled, the girls' hair a mess, the boys' pants falling down, shoes missing, socks gone, sweaters lost, and they were very, very wet. Many went to bed that night with the ague already coming on. The mistress was terribly angry, and she forbade the children to walk to the pond ever again.

But, then, they never asked.

Eventually, they all grew up and left the orphanage, and as they wandered the world creating themselves—a hard task for any of us and a harder one for orphans— each looked for a three-story house with double doors that opened onto a wraparound verandah upon which sat wicker furniture. They looked for a fat, furry cat stretched on the banister, a cat with a tail that teased the flowers, and for a spotted dog at the porch steps waiting to be whistled. The people they imagined sitting in the wicker furniture, sipping lemonade and eating chocolate-chip cookies, were themselves.

All of the children—even the one with the withered leg and the other with no sight—married and had babies. And while their spouses desired names like Millicent and Arthur and Christopher and Isadora, the former orphans were adamant in calling their boys Joey and their girls Babby. When asked why, they simply claimed they were old family names. All the parents loved their joeys and their babbies very much. And not one beloved ran away to live beneath the ice.

A Mother Writes a Letter to Her Son

14TH JUNE
Steen—

I'm sitting with one of the photo albums, looking at a snap of you and your dad. You're no more than two, mud-coated like some bog child, and you're grinning and staring straight ahead, your arm stretched to the camera, your little fist offering me a soggy twig that dangles between your fingers, as if exchanges were easy, as if you don't even have to care very much, as if all your barters will be accepted.

Your dad presses you tightly to his side, muddying the front and arms of his coat, despite his hatred of dirt. He does not look at the camera but studies you, his face close to yours, studies you with your curly brown hair and apple cheeks, he with his straight, thin, blond hair; his straight, thin face; his pale skin. Though he is in profile and looks down, you can see that he smiles with the delight he always has when he watches you. He still does, even now that you're a grown man. Behind the two of you, the hills that stretch to the Buckle Summit are green and velvety, and above them, clouds drift like small, remaining floes of winter across the blue sky.

"Look at you," I like to remember saying. "You little philistine!" And I snapped the picture and then changed the phrase just slightly: "Phil's steen!"

Your dad looked up at me then, so pleased that I had called you his, that you were named after him and that your relationship was secure enough that you could be teased about your name, and that, finally, you were so eager to immerse yourself in the nitty-gritty of the world. Your dad seldom laughs out loud, but that spring day he did when he said, "He looks more chocolate than mud-coated." What he meant, of course, was that to him you were exquisite and sweet and beautiful.

Since that day twenty-four years ago, we've called you Steen instead of Phil. It has been a better name.

Other than the story about Phillip morphing to Philistine morphing to Phil's steen, then to Steen, other than the story of some wordplay on a pretty spring day, you've never heard the context that day fits into. I suppose that's why we like snapshots. They're pared down and made simple; nothing but white space surrounds them, and when we look back on these incremental images of our lives, our lives seem simple, too. And happy. The context we've forgotten or chosen to forget. But sometimes the white space between snapshots—between then and now—begins to fill in, and we're shocked, because we haven't expected it. I know I haven't. And Phillip hasn't expected it, either. And but for you, we might have been able to keep it that way.

Perhaps we still can, but I am frightened that when you encounter him on your rounds at the nursing home in the next week, you will sense his importance to you, and, because you are like your mother—left-handed and right-brained, paying attention to intuition—you will wonder at this feeling you have, and you will honor it; and because you are like your father, with his accountant's belief that the truth can be found in data, that one has only to be aware of the need to find it and record it and examine it, you will search for data to explain your feeling.

We have always been so proud of you, Steen, for balancing in yourself so well our warring personalities. It is no wonder that you have become a physician, a healer, for you intuit the discomfort of people and then diagnose its cause.

How ironic that what thrilled us—your return to Buckle to do a residency and reduce your med school debt by doing duty in a rural community—might undo what your father and I have worked so hard to protect you from. Might undo you. Might undo us all.

I wondered about returning to Buckle when Dad and I graduated from college and you were three, because, as in any small town, gossip abounds, and gossip never revolves around people's secret virtues. Even though we had been married for almost three years by then, I felt coming home might once again start people talking about what an odd match your dad and I were, might start them talking again about our shotgun wedding, about how Phil didn't seem the type to get a girl—let alone me—pregnant. On this we have always been honest with you; you know that we married when I was six months pregnant, and we have always told you that you were wanted by both of us. So wanted.

And this seemed enough—that you were wanted. Your dad convinced me that if we kept the context secret and our countenances open, we would live securely in the world of Buckle. And we have.

But yesterday we heard that Fergus Meagher has come home. "He's back," your dad said, in as nonchalant a way as he could, and he didn't have to give his name; I would know because, even though we have pretended otherwise, Fergus Meagher has never left. He has always been here.

And now, because he will live at the nursing home, you will meet him. I don't know what he will look like. I don't know if, as stroke victims often do, he will have deadened, twisted features. All I know is that people who have had brain-stem strokes maintain their ability to receive information; they just struggle disseminating what it is they know. And I don't know what he knows, or if he will be able to tell you anything.

At first I prayed that he is terribly deformed, that you will look on him and see nothing resembling . . . what shall I say . . . a man? A human being? What a terrible thing to wish on another, but I did. I thought that if he has been afflicted by a terrible twist of fate and face, then there would be a chance that you would never see this letter. Sometime next week, you would drop by and tell us that there is a new patient at the facility, the youngest son of the Meagher family, the one Phil and I went to school with, the one who has been living in California, the one about whom gossip abounds. You coyly ask me if I, like every other woman in Buckle, have seen one of his films, and I tell you no, even as I blush, but not for the reason you think.

But if he is not transformed into some lost creature, you may look at him and feel a resonance in you, because the face pinning you with its gaze reveals a chastening secret.

How you might hate us should that happen. And, so, ironically, I will assure your hatred by telling you the secret now. It is, after all, only fair. I think I've always known I should tell you, but I've been so thankful to your father, and he has never wanted this divulged. While I've loved your father, like any mother I've loved you more, and with each year that you have grown, so has my love. It would be remiss of me not to forewarn one I love so dearly of danger, which Fergus Meagher clearly represents.

Your father and I have always had what you doctors call unremarkable histories. And for years, you have assumed that you have inherited this genetic encoding that allows you to be, in this one area alone, unremarkable. And I'm sure you've looked at both sides of the family and been grateful for such normalcy. I pray, of course, that this failure to excel at illness remains. But this stroke of a man you've never met could suggest otherwise.

———

I LOOK BACK at what I struggle to write, Steen. Four pages. Do you remember that old joke you used to tell over and over about the young man who calls home from college to see how everyone is, and his little sister tells him his cat died? He gets angry at her for being so blunt and tells her she should have broken this news to him gently by first explaining how the cat was up a tree and they couldn't get it down. When he called again, he should have been told the cat was still in the tree and weakening, and when he called again, expecting dire straits, he could have been told that the cat had died. The little sister apologizes for her insensitivity. A week later, when the young man calls home and gets his sister, he asks how everyone is. "Mom's up a tree, and we can't get her down," the sister tells him. This is what I'm doing. Stalling the truth. And you, no doubt, have already surmised what that is.

YOU KNOW the Meaghers; both men and women are handsome. They are tall and well proportioned, ruddy in complexion, blue of eye, and topped with auburn curls. Even the men, with their angular features and muscular bodies, are softened by ringlets. To a degree, they have been distrusted by the town; it's not because they seldom come to Buckle—many ranch families come in just once a week; and it's not because most of them still live on the old homestead—a quality of feudalism still functions on many of the ranches in the Buckle Valley, if the holdings are large enough; and it's not because they're Mormon—half the valley is that, and why should we distrust them anymore than the Catholics or Methodists? I suspect it is their steadfast handsomeness which makes most of Buckle, when they look at the Meaghers, seem unfinished, as if God was still experimenting on features and body shapes, as if He'd been shaping their clay forms with the hands of an amateur till he got to the Meaghers. And only then was He pleased. So pleased that He forgot to squash the imperfect experiments and start anew, to make each creation as perfect. And so the people of the Buckle Valley limp and shuffle around, too pudgy and too thin, bowlegged and knock-kneed, splay-footed and pigeon-toed, all the while envying the Meaghers.

What's more, the Meaghers' physical perfection doesn't fade. You know this because Reba Meagher is one of your patients at the home; though she hasn't a thought left in her head, she's still stunning. It doesn't fade through the generations, either. The Meaghers seem incapable of throwing an ugly child.

After all, look at you.

And there you have it. The truth.

I KNOW what you are doing now; I used to watch how you read—intently, with your nose not more than twelve inches from the page, even though there is no flaw in your ability to see; and after a few pages you stop and stare into space, the blue of your eyes stormy with words and then calming as they become moored in the fine harbor of your mind. Only when all the words are anchored do you return to reading, and your eyes storm again. And perhaps I should be quiet now and just let you settle this idea. But I am so frightened of losing you that I will keep writing, trying to hold on to you.

WE ARE SO OPTIMISTIC, we humans. No, let me rephrase that: we try so hard to be optimistic. Drunks believe a new day is a new beginning; most of us pretend that a new year erases the old, that new habits will write themselves into new calendars we receive as Christmas presents; all of us embrace a baby as a new life with its own story to make. I know I certainly did.

But what I now understand is that babies are merely new characters in a plot already unwinding, a plot that began with Adam and Eve; I think they were the only two people ever allowed to start a story. What would they have done differently had they had the foresight to understand this? What would any of us do? And perhaps that, more than our mortality, is our punishment: it is only after we have lost our youth, our impetuosity, only after we have lived a while and garnered, if not wisdom then at least consequences, that we understand how fully, and sometimes how terribly, we have affected the plot.

I MET FERGUS MEAGHER in eighth grade, when he couldn't go to the school at Smelt anymore. I think that one-room school has stayed open because of the Meaghers—there are always so many brothers and sisters, and so many cousins! He was the youngest of Reba's and Lem's kids.

When he came to Buckle High, I was a moon-eyed girl, in love with poetry, in love with love, and when I saw Fergus, who was so beautiful, I was sure he had been named for the mythic king of Yeats's poetry. In truth, as they had for all their children, Reba and Lem had turned to the state map and chosen a county name. But for Fergus, you've met them all at the nursing home when they come to visit their mother: Lewis, Carter, Clark, Judith, Bonner, Dawson, and Cassia. All counties. Every last one of them.

I remember studying Fergus from my desk the first day he came in, and Kate Brethwaite—Miss Brethwaite to me then—who was our homeroom teacher, introduced him to us. He stood there still as a statue, except for his hands, which twirled an old felt hat round and round, and the pointy, duct-taped toe of one cowboy boot, which tapped the floor. He was an odd combination of vulnerability and impatience—like a caged animal, I thought. That day, every girl in the class fell in love with him. I think even Miss Brethwaite—who was indomitable then—fell. While we girls sat and stared transfixed, the boys—even your kind dad—turned away from him; they excluded him for the next four years.

Not long after he arrived, Fergus and I became best friends. Perhaps it was because the boys would have nothing to do with him and most of the girls were too shy to approach him. Oh, just like everyone else, I thought he was beautiful, but I liked him more for his connection to the poetry I loved, the poetry I've read to you through the years. You know it all, Steen. And some he fit so perfectly! Remember "a king and proud! and that is my despair" from "Fergus and the Druid"? Of course it was only high school in a small western town, but when I thought of how Fergus was treated by everyone, of how he kept his pride in the solitude the students forced upon him, he became in my imagination that Irish king, and all I wanted was to befriend him.

And that's really all it was, a friendship, a great friendship, in which we did everything together. We snuck our first cigarettes together, drank our first illegal beer together, smoked our first weed together, necked and fondled together. We committed these acts in haystacks on various ranches surrounding Buckle; everyone still used the old beaverslide method of stacking, and we would scurry up the big green loaves with a blanket in the evenings and lie in the heady blue blossoms of alfalfa and stars. Truly, Steen, it had not been any kind of emotion that drove us but the lasered curiosity of inexperience coupled with a spacious comfort made of both landscape and familiarity, the same kind of curiosity I suspect you shared with Abigail your senior year of high school. We would trace the outlines of each other's bodies with a studiousness, more biologists than lovers.

I remember once sitting with him on top of a haystack watching the sun melt into the warm September horizon and waiting for the sigh of the finished day that would cool the world. "You know that Keats poem we're doing in English, about the Grecian urn?"

"You mean the one that doesn't make any sense?" Fergus asked. I think he was angry because he'd wanted to study my anatomy further than I would allow, and he was trying to provoke me. "Beauty is truth and truth beauty, and that's all I need to know? I need to know a lot more than that. I hate that poem. I've seen things that are true, and they sure aren't pretty."

I wasn't thinking about that part of the poem at all, but I was impressed that Fergus, who was straightforward and direct—not one to remember lines of poetry— knew them, so I asked, "Like what?"

"Like watching cows have sex. Like chopping chicken heads off. Like cracking an egg open and having a bloody chick fall out. Like having to shoot a horse that's broke its leg. Like like like. You want me to go on?"

You're probably wondering how I can so exactly remember this, but, in this case, I do, because I was using "Ode on a Grecian Urn" to keep my virginity, and the part of the poem I meant was where Keats says that the figures on the urn will never catch each other, and that makes life better. And I, shaped by the ambition that a scholarship would be my ticket out of Buckle, recited,

Bold Lover, never, never canst thou kiss,
Though winning near the goal—yet, do not grieve;
She cannot fade, though thou hast not thy bliss,
Forever wilt thou love, and she be fair!

What I was trying to tell Fergus was that he and I could never love fully. You must understand that I was seventeen, and I thought having sex was tantamount to loving fully, and I couldn't do that because I so desperately wanted out of Buckle, and I knew if I loved Fergus fully, I might get pregnant, and then I'd never be able to leave. My life, which in my sweet youth I thought should be informed by poetry, would end up being prosaic.

The irony, of course, is that, as you know, I did get a scholarship. And because I did and had escaped Buckle, I believed myself immune to everything prosaic. When Fergus stopped on his way to Los Angeles to become a stuntman in the movies, then I let him in. The figures kissed, and more. Just that once, Steen.

NOW THIS SOUNDS like a letter of apology to the child of that brief union. I don't mean it to. How could I ever be sorry for you!

But understand that at the beginning of my college education, which I believed would take me to all the places I had imagined, I rued the pregnancy. At Christmas of my freshman year, I went home, saying nothing to your grandparents or aunt, watching the days during which I could get an abortion—if only I knew how and where—wind down. That new year, when I returned for my second semester, I realized what I have earlier told you: that there are no new beginnings. The story was in play, and there would be no stopping it.

What I didn't yet accept was that I was the story's author. And this is where I let your father—not Fergus, but your father, your real one, the one who has adored you all these years—enter the plot.

Just as I loved Fergus through high school, Phillip loved me. Though he was too shy to act on his affection, I could tell. I remember one snowy day complaining to your grandmother that he loved me, and I knew it, and everyone else knew it, too, and it was embarrassing. Everything about him was thin and pale—the back pockets of his Levi's drooped around his buttocks, his shoulders rounded over a chest that seemed concave, his hair had a see-through blondness to it, and it was not thick so that when he failed to wash it, you could see his white scalp, and his face was long and pulled on his lips, giving him a constant look of bereavement. He was not the kind of boy girls wanted to be loved by.

"Phillip Steen likes me," I told Mama. "Too much." She and your aunt Alice and I were sitting around the old kitchen table, the one Mama and Daddy still use, the one scarred by previous owners. You know the story, how along with that table and some other old furniture, the ranch came with anecdotes, and when we moved onto it, we cozied into them—both the furniture and the stories. The table, from the cookhouse, had been signed by Lyle. Do you remember how you used to trace his name with your fork whenever Mama made you macaroni and cheese and broccoli? Then you'd try to divert our attention by asking to hear his story again—how long before even I was born, he had blown his hands off with dynamite and so wore two silver hooks, and how he scratched away with whatever hook he wrote with until, eventually, *Lyle* appeared. His name, deepened by your tracing, still floats on the table like a soul on a Ouija board.

I remember Mama glancing at me as she slid a piece of lodgepole into the woodstove. "How could anyone like you too much? You're worthy of all the affection you receive." She dropped the iron latch on the firebox. "You should be flattered that such a nice boy likes you."

Alice and I looked at each other and rolled our eyes when Mama said, "He's good to have in a crowd of kids. He's like the piece of green cottonwood you throw into the cookstove to calm the fire." Neither of us was interested in boys who cooled. We were after boys of willow or aspen, boys of fast and fierce heat.

Despite my dismay over Phillip's constant crush on me, I used him in my math and science classes because he was so smart. Without him, my grades, though strong in the humanities, wouldn't have been well-rounded enough to get my scholarship. And I like to think that without my help in his essays, Phillip wouldn't have received his. At any rate, we were habituated to each other's company, and at college, though less often, we still met to help one another.

It was during one of those meetings in February. We were sitting in the library, and I had just pointed out a sentence in an essay he was working on for a philosophy class—problems of good and evil. There was nothing wrong with the sentence except for what it said—at least for me. Phillip had written, "Our culture panders to a morbid interest in our misdeeds; we create trouble just for the pleasure of wallowing in it."

"That's not true," I said. I was, of course, thinking of myself, of my own troubles, and how there was no pleasure in them, and because I knew he loved me, it was easy to take it out on Phillip. I crossed his lines out, pressing so hard that the pencil ripped his paper in half.

Then I pushed it back to him, crumpling it.

Calmly he straightened it out and wrote for just a moment before handing it to me again. "Are you pregnant?" it asked.

In embarrassment that I must be showing and in relief that I could finally talk to someone about my state, I leaned into his shoulder, my eyes pressed against his thin shoulder blade, and sobbed. I will always remember the firmness and the gentleness of his hand as it stroked the back of my head. I will always remember how mature it felt, and how even as I welcomed its touch, it was not the kind of touch I longed for. But I would learn.

You, of course, have heard part of this story, and while we never lied, we let you assume that that evening in the library, a young man was being informed of his own potency instead of someone else's.

A month later, we were married at the courthouse and went home to announce our marriage and your impending birth. Both of our families were disappointed.

Of course, when they saw you, their disappointment disappeared. You were beautiful, and everyone talked with amazement at the nicking of two average looking people, dumbfounded that our ho-hum genes—at least as far as looks go—would come together to create such perfection.

DO YOU REMEMBER how you used to ask me why we didn't have a brother or sister for you to play with?

As I grew fond of your father's touch, I wanted to have more children—not for you, but for us—but so proud was he of you, and of the fiction that you were his, that he refused to consider it. "What if the baby looks like me?" he'd ask.

It has been a deep disappointment to me that you were an only child; but more than that, it has been a deep sadness to me that your father has so doubted the kind of beauty he has that when we have made love, it has never been complete. Always separating us has been .05 millimeter of latex. Only when my fecundity has ended will your father fully love me.

The deepest sadness of all, however, my beloved Steen, is that with this letter, you will never look on us again with the love we have come to expect on your face.

I don't know if I can bear that loss. I don't know if I can bear to change the myth of your life that we have created. I don't know if I can give you this. I don't know. I don't know.

The Skater

For John Cheever

Most sundays after another morning of feeding live-stock and another sermon by Reverend Starr, everyone, in one way or another, said, "I'm bored." It was whispered by the parishioners leaving the Buckle Community Church, and they imagined it even coming from the lips of the old preacher himself as his wife struggled to unbutton the starched backward collar from his wrinkled chicken neck; it was heard from the salesmen reading an issue of last year's Time in the lobby at the Buckle River Inn, heard from the staff at the Carnegie Library who would rather not work on Sunday but knew there was nothing else for anyone—even them—to do, heard from the ranchers and their families in their tall white houses, heard from the hired men playing solitaire together in the bunkhouses, heard from the horses who wandered in circles, noses to the frozen mud and lips quivering above every stray piece of hay or straw in the corrals, heard from the cattle hanging over the green line of alfalfa and grass tossed out to them, more ready to be slaughtered than spend another gray day doing nothing but staying alive.

But this Sunday was also the winter solstice, and a full-moon one at that. It meant that that night, at the edge of the Mulkeys' pond, there would be a big bonfire around which many of the community would gather.

THE POND, frozen solid since Thanksgiving, was supplied by an artesian well with a high iron content, so the ice was green; it was also etched by the blades of skates, smeared by the plastic trays from the high school's cafeteria, and tracked by the aluminum legs of summer lawn chairs pushed across it. It was a fine night. In the east the moon, yellow and magnified, rose above Buckle Summit, coming at them like the headlight of a locomotive and diminishing the drama of the flames and sparks that shot from the bonfire that had been lit. The burn pile was huge, as over the last week everyone had brought the unused stumps and boughs of the evergreens they'd cut for Christmas, the fireplace logs too big to split even with a wedge, milk cartons and newspapers and magazines and medical bills they wanted to forget about. And many, to the consternation of Reverend Starr, had come with scraps of paper on which they'd written their failures and planned to throw into the flames—as if redemption could be found in fire and soot rather than in prayer. On other scraps, hopes had been written, which made no sense at all: to send your hopes up in smoke before you even got a chance to act on them.

The night was cold. Kate Brethwaite sat by the fire in a lawn chair. She was a big woman—tall and thick-boned and heavy breasted—and while she was far from old, she had an air of authority and gravity, enhanced not only by her physique but by her position in Buckle: she was the physics teacher at the valley's consolidated high school. So seriously did she take her job that one day, taped to the bruised wooden door behind which she taught what she believed to be the wonders of the universe, was a doctored picture; upon the body of a uniformed policeman with a threatening billy club sat her head, copied from the yearbook. Under her frowning face, which many whispered resembled George Washington's, someone had scrawled: "Obey gravity. It's the law." She had been skating, and now she was breathing deeply, as if she could fill her chest with the elements of the moment: the bonfire heating the wool of her jacket and the sweater beneath that and her skin beneath that, while her back was penetrated by cold and the moon that frigidly stared through her clothes to her spine and the goose bumps running down it . . . an intensity of chaos she intellectually knew existed but seldom felt. It was this fleeting sense of disorderliness that made her think, as she watched everyone skate and slide and get pushed in lawn chairs in a circle around the pond, that by following the moon east across the hummocky field about two hundred feet, she would come to Mulkey Slough, no doubt frozen as solidly as the pond. Under the illumination of the moon, she could skate approximately five miles to where the Buckle River fed the slough and past which the town of Buckle rested. At the river, she would have to leave the ice and trudge across the bridge, walk to Main, and go another two blocks to her home. There Albert and Elsa, her two Siamese cats, littermates named after her hero Albert Einstein and his first cousin and second wife, Elsa, would be sleeping on her over-stuffed chairs in front of the woodstove she'd stoked just before leaving for the solstice party. She looked down at the men's hockey skates she wore—the only skates at the Buckle Mercantile large enough to fit her size eleven feet—and rolled her stalwart ankles, testing them.

Though almost everyone in Buckle, an informal little dot on the map, called one another by their first names, they continued to call Kate "Miss Brethwaite," despite the fact that she'd been in the community for a decade. While it should have bothered her, she decided this stiffness of the citizens toward her was not ostracism—something that often happens to outsiders in small towns—but recognition of the constant quality of education she dispensed. In short, she did not view her life as lonely, so the pleasure she took in contemplating skating home could not be explained as any sort of aloofness on her part. With the eye of a Lewis or Clark who two hundred years earlier had come upstream just a few miles to the south, she visualized the man-made slough that curved across the land. Like those fearless discoverers, she would travel by water—or, in this case, ice—to a destination she was sure of. Her twin bed. And once classes resumed after the new year, she could tell her students of her journey, and she knew that while a few might laugh at her, most would recognize her as the imaginative figure she saw herself to be. The night was glorious, and it seemed to her that such a unique, long skate would magnify its perfection.

She stood up, wobbling just a little on the thin blades, buttoned the top two buttons of her wool coat, pulled the collar up, yanked her stocking cap down, and turned from the pond and its Brueghelian business. As she carefully navigated the hummocks of the Mulkeys' field, she felt the heat of the fire recede from her chest, to be replaced by an omnipotent shiver that forked at her sternum, flicking like a frigid flame to each of her nipples, scorching them in a cold heat. At that very moment, she thought, they must be as big and pulsating and alive as two stars. To be embraced like that, to be awakened physically by the cosmos whose laws always so excited her mind, was such a pleasure that she considered stripping her clothes off so that by the time she got to the slough she could glide through the night buck naked. This, however, was not possible, considering the length of her journey and the temperature of the evening. When Fergus Meagher, one of her students—the only student she ever had had a crush on even though he was so awful at physics—asked her where she was going, she flirtatiously answered she was skating home. She did not look back to see the look on his face, but she was sure it was admiring.

Her only hesitation came when she had to step down the steep rolled bank of terra firma to the ice of the slough, which unwound to the north like a two-toned ribbon, half of it a luminescent yellow of reflected moon, the other half, in the shadow of the far bank, a dark gray that threatened to usurp the light of the other side. When finally she stood in the middle of the slough, wiping the snow from her bottom because she'd decided to slide down the bank, she let her eye follow the icy trail she'd committed to. Her knees already felt a little weary, and when she looked down, she noticed that one skate looked gold in the moonlight; the other was drowned in darkness. She took a deep breath; there was no map or chart to figure out, no false channel or river to follow; there was no need to worry. The night was lovely, and that she lived in a world so brimming with sky and moon and stars and ice felt divinely beneficent. A scientist, she ruefully smiled at her acknowledgement of the divine. But who knew, really? Kate Brethwaite's heart was high, and she pushed off with the long blade of her moonlit left foot. Making her way home in an unusual way reinforced that she was at best an explorer and at worst a pilgrim. In either case, she was a woman who this night had a destiny to fulfill.

She was stopped by three strands of barbed wire that separated, she supposed, the Mulkeys' land from the neighbor's, and she saw in her mind's eye Highway 29, which ran through Buckle Valley, and the ranch houses that in the summer humped out of the grassy meadows like whales—great Moby-Dicks—in a green ocean. Down from the Mulkeys were the Clydes. So now she was on Clyde land. Once she had threaded her way through the wire, she ducked under the naked branches of a stand of willows that overhung the slough, feeling them scratch at the back of her coat and pull at her hat. Leaves and twigs, frozen in the ice, made an indecipherable calligraphy she was forced to slowly study, as the blades of her skates refused to slip easily over the foreign letters made by nature, forcing her to take tiny baby steps. She saw then, like any traveler, that even the most unthreatening of routes would have inhospitable and untranslatable elements that would have to be handled with care if she was going to reach her destination. She did not want to exaggerate the barriers of first barbed wire and now willows, but given the temperature, she was aware that there would be no time to linger over the mysterious alphabet imprinted in the ice, and what she loved most was translating mystery. Within thirty feet, she could straighten again and, brushing her shoulders of twigs and shaking out her hat and pulling it down tightly again, she skated away. She went by three cottonwood trees that cast shadows across the slough. A doe, bedded down, looked up and watched her skate by, unsure of what she was; but she was quiet and quick and smooth enough that before the deer could think to startle, she was past. Not far from that, a hefty branch of another cottonwood had fallen across the slough. Slowly she crawled up the bank to go around it, hearing somewhere above and beyond it the reassuring lowing and the incessant chewing of cud by cattle.

The cold air first heightened their sounds and then froze them in midair. She topped the bank and stood. Her ankles, while steady with momentum on the ice, wobbled, and she felt her toes cramp. Straightening and placing her thumbs in the small of her back, she stretched and surveyed how far she might have to trek on the land, which rose and then dipped away to where the cows could be seen, their bottoms pressed together against the cold and the night, facing outward to watch for any danger. Oh, how kind and thoughtful was the life along the slough! Kate felt the start of a sob in her chest, a reaction to the scene, a tenderness for this modest gathering of life, as if it were something she could touch. The world darkened for just a moment as a cloud scudded in front of the moon. As if the shadow foretold of a threat, a cow lifted its drooped head. Seeing Kate's outline, it bawled and took one and then another step toward her, rousing the whole mandala, who fell out of their cosmic configuration and lined up in a defensive maneuver. "I'm sorry," Kate said to them, hoping her voice would assure them she was human and no danger—at least until the fall, when humans would take them to a feedlot to be prepared for slaughter. "I mean you no harm." And she thought again of Lewis and Clark, as they wended and yawed their way westward, looking for the Pacific, telling tribes of Indians, "We mean you no harm." She toddled in her skates around the end of the fallen cottonwood, a mittened hand dragging along the scaly bark. With the other, she gestured to the line of cattle that now walked her way, either to attack her or to wait for hay they equated with the human form and voice. When she seemed about to be surrounded, she had nearly completed her detour, so she dropped onto her bottom and slid quickly down the bank, safe on the ice of the slough.

Standing once again, with a broad smile, she pushed off and off and again and again, quickly attaining a rhythmic glide that her breathing soon accompanied. As the solid blue slid easily beneath her so that she dizzied, unsure if she was propelling herself forward or some force pulled the ribbon of ice beneath her, unsure except for the feel of her muscles in her thighs and the swinging of her arms and the heightened beating of her heart, the bawling of the cows muted and then softened and then dissipated into the silence of the night. As she slid along, Kate watched the landscape flow by, uninterrupted, until she came to the large form of a tall, white two-story house yellowed by the moonlight. In the vast landscape, it looked out of place and confined, darkened except for one window on the second floor, where someone watched television. The light of the cathode rays flickered artificially against the lively light of the stars and moon. Beyond that, there were no signs of life—not even a dog barking. Sunday night in the Buckle Valley. The thought tired her a little, but once around a curve of the slough and away from the house, she felt clean, clean and pleased, pleased to be by herself alone, pleased by everything.

It was darkening. The one scud of cloud that earlier crossed the moon had been followed by another, and then by a thickening band. What time, she wondered, had it gotten to be? Eight? Nine? She glanced at her watch; the moonlight that remained made it too light for its face to glow, yet the night was too dark for her to read the dial. A train whistle blew, once, twice, growing louder as it came at her and then again and again as it went away from her, and Kate thought about the Doppler effect, a principle in physics that says a sound coming at you is louder than the same sound going away from you, and she thought about morning, about tomorrow, and how it would come at her even as this day left. She thought about how when dusk came the few birds lunatic enough to stay the winter in the Buckle Valley organized their songs into an acute silence in recognition of the day's going. Just then there was a fine noise of rushing air from the crown of a cottonwood at her back, as if someone much larger than she had sighed, and a breeze rustled her cap. Then hoots came from the crowns of two other tall trees. Owls. Why did they love the night? What was the meaning of the talk they made when the door of the sky sprang open and the darkness tumbled down the stairs to the earth? Why did their flight seem both languid but urgent? Why did their hollow harmonies have for her the unmistakable sound of sad tidings? Then the owl landed on a branch in front of her, not twenty feet away. Its eyes caught the moonlight and reflected it on her, two small laser beams momentarily burning her.

She did not move until the owl lifted, and her stillness had cooled her and she shivered. Though owls in the night were fitting, she had felt a familiar sadness in their presence. But she shook her shivers off like a dog does water from its coat and, bracing her shoulders, she once again pushed off, visualizing whose land beyond the Clydes' she would skate through, the prospect of what would come next reinvigorating her. Once again, the moon had cleared. No cataract of cloud dimmed it.

———

HAD YOU BEEN headed west on Highway 29 that night, you might have seen her, bearlike in her coat, waiting in the shadow of an abutment to cross the narrow two-lane bridge over the Buckle River. You might have wondered if her car had slid off the road into the borrow ditch on her way home, or if she was a homeless person driven by the dark and the cold to come out of some ramshackle den, or if, because of her skates, she was just a fool. Standing next to the artless graffiti—*CP Is An Ass, TS Hearts LN, Life Is Ticking Away TickTock, Fuck U*—she seemed pathetic to herself. When she had started her journey, she had not considered this—it hadn't been on her maps—but confronted with the image of her waddling across the bridge and rocking like an ogre that lived underneath it, and then getting pinned like a deer in the headlights of some approaching car, she found herself unprepared. So she waited and wondered what time it was and how many people would still be out driving, and she counted cars and the seconds it took them to cross the bridge, and she calculated how much time she would need to cross it and drop down into the borrow ditch before another came along. She considered going back, back to Mulkeys' pond, rewinding her actions, the ribbon of slough now like the ribbon of a Möbius strip she had hung in her class to show students how confused space and time were, so that she would arrive and it would be just as she had left it—the sapphire pond, the revelers upon it spinning and circling and laughing and talking, the fire heating them and casting embers to the moon in hubristic challenge. Yes, she could go back. She had promised nothing, said nothing, except to Fergus Meagher. And that beautiful boy was too quiet to say anything.

Why, believing as she did, that the world was subject to physical laws, laws that she perhaps of all the citizens of Buckle understood, did she not turn back? Why was she going to finish her journey even if it meant being seen crossing the bridge and losing her reputation in the community? At what point had this lark become serious? For, however long it had taken her, she had covered a distance that now made going back impossible.

A pickup, slowing down to twenty miles an hour, rumbled onto the bridge. She recognized the five bobbing blobs in it as the heads of the Steens; Phillip, a pimply boy with thick glasses and wobbly eyeballs, was her star pupil this year. She groaned at the thought of him spotting her. Next to cross was a semi, and the vibrations caused in the bridge's structure by its weight and the application of its jake brakes rattled her heart into action. As quickly as she could—which was not at all—she herringboned and panted up the slope of frozen slush to the bare highway, feeling as if all strength in her thighs was gone. Hurriedly she crossed as the sound of the truck's engines and the sight of its taillights grew smaller and then winked out, her ankles bending first in and then out with each step made. As she listened for the hiss of tires on tar and watched the reflectors for any sign of headlights and hunched along like Quasimodo, she began to cry. But there was no traffic, and she wiped her eyes as she dropped with relief into the ditch.

It had been a long time since she cried; she tried to

remember when that had been and thought it to be at her cat Tycho Brahe's death fourteen years earlier. But even then, she was not as sad and bewildered, or as cold, as she was this night. She had skated too long, she had breathed in too heavily the ice crystals of the night, and her nose ran and her throat stung and her chest ached. She was tired. So tired.

From here, she had a quarter mile—how could she have forgotten it was so far—to Main Street, and then the two blocks home. She stumbled down the borrow ditch filled with the detritus of the world—beer and pop cans, wads of paper, truckers' piss bombs, twisted rags, blowout patches of rubber—and thought of the green ice at the Mulkeys' with longing and wondered if she would be defiled by this muck she was slogging through. But she told herself that she was a pilgrim, an explorer, and that this was merely a corrupt section of her journey. She grimaced with distaste as she stepped around the desiccated head of a deer. When the first street lamp of Buckle grew from the rim of land she stumbled beneath, she dropped down onto her hands and knees and crawled up the bank; panting, she peered both ways for traffic and ducked as a car slowly pulled onto Main Street and crept toward where she crouched. It was the old dinosaur Cadillac of Linus Anglin, and Kate considered stepping out and hailing him as people in cities did taxis.

Linus was an elderly man, the retired president of the Stockman Bank who seemed to delight in the imperviousness that a certain age and a modicum of wealth had given him. To be stopped in the dark by the physics teacher at the Buckle Valley Consolidated High School, whose consolidation came into being when he served on the school board, would gratify him, and he would be amused by her tale of skating home; even better, by morning he would have forgotten all about it. But he would have to somehow turn the car around, and she imagined his U-turn taking forever and one of the Cadillac's fins hitting the trunk of one of the cottonwood trees that welcomed visitors into Buckle and Wyatt Heath, the deputy sheriff out trolling for tipsy people returning from the solstice party, investigating . . . She watched Linus go by, so shrunken that his head was barely visible above the window. And she had only a little more than two blocks to go to finish the journey of her own will. Plus, there were plenty of trees to duck behind if any cars should come.

She looked at the single-storied buildings huddled ahead of her, dark except for the yellow moonlight that reflected off their windows and siding, belying a liveliness they lacked. She smelled the stubborn winter fragrance of smoke and ice on the night air. Hobbling along, staggering with fatigue through the clotted shadows of the cottonwoods, she wondered if she would have the strength to go these last blocks. She had done what she wanted, she had skated the landscape over, but she was so dazed with exhaustion that her victory was lost to her. Stooped and on occasion leaning against the trees not to hide but to stay upright, she finally arrived at her own home. She saw that the fire had burned out, as no smoke escaped her chimney, and as she opened the low picket gate she thought how cold it would be inside.

The house was dark. Had she forgotten to turn a light

on before leaving? She climbed the steps of the porch and turned the knob of the door, but it was locked. How had this happened? One of the reasons she'd accepted a job in Buckle was because one needn't lock one's house. She went from window to window, rattling them, but they were hinged tight against the winter. Returning to the door, she pounded on it, and finally she pushed at it with her shoulder, for she knew neither Albert nor Elsa would ever open it and let her in.

Acknowledgments

A story isn't complete until someone reads it. And I have come to understand that "finishing" a story in this way—getting it to an audience—is the grueling part. That you have been able to read these stories is in large part due to my agent Sandra Bond, a petite woman with a gargantuan will. Without her, this collection would still be sitting in a drawer in my computer.

Of course, to find an agent like Sandra, I first had to be "legitimate." Helping with my legitimacy has been Deborah O'Connor, the editor for a score of years at *Northern Lights*, a journal out of Missoula, Montana, which gained national prestige by the quality of writing it offered. Deb is one of the most generous people I've ever met; when she found work she liked, she did everything she could to promote it, submitting to venues that would help validate a writer: for me, it was the Pushcart Prize and the Rona Jaffe Foundation. Armed with a portfolio and a couple of awards, then, I had the confidence to go in search of an agent like Sandra.

An interesting aspect—a reward, I'd say—of writing professionally is that one becomes friends with people without having "met" them. This was the case with Sandra and Deb. I did not meet Sandra face-to-face until a year after she took me on. I did not meet Deb for two years after she first published my work.

With this book, I have made more friends in such a way. Christopher Lehmann-Haupt, the editorial director at Delphinium Books, is one of them. Christopher has been critical but kind, coaxing me into more precise language and tighter stories. And then there is Carl Lennertz, Vice President of Independent Retailing at HarperCollins; he's been the strategist, the front man, the enthusiastic hawker of this book, the one who has placed it so readers could find it, take it home, and finish the stories for me.

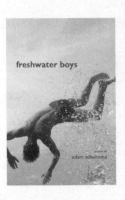